"Should I know you?"

Julianne asked, swallowing hard.

"Probably not. I'm a simple mountain guide." He bowed slightly. "Erich Langlois."

The breath lodged in her lungs. "Are you related to—" she almost said the resident ghost, then thought better of it "—Frederick Langlois?"

"My most infamous ancestor. A witch, they say, who tinkered with curses and assorted incantations." He leaned toward her, so close his breath was a wisp of warmth across her cheek, more imagined than felt. "The village gossips claim he could cause warts to grow on the end of a virgin's nose."

"You're terrible!"

"And irreverent," he conceded. His lips slid into a smile—a wicked smile—and Julianne knew she was in danger of losing her heart to this dark, dangerous man who could so easily cast a spell over her. Or had he already?

Dear Reader,

Ever wonder what it would be like to meet not one
but *four* fabulous handsome hunks? Well, you're
about to find out! Four of the most fearless, strong
and sexy men are brought to their knees by the
undeniable power of love—in this month's special
VALENTINE'S MEN.

Meet Erich Langlois, mountain climber
extraordinaire, in Charlotte Maclay's
The Bewitching Bachelor. After a trip to
Austria, Charlotte came back all aglow, with
this story firmly planted in her brain. She had
little to say about the matter, as her charming
and oh-so-sexy hero refused to rest until his
story was told and the Langlois name
was cleared.

We don't want you to miss out on any of these sexy
guys, so be sure to check out *all* the titles in our
special VALENTINE'S MEN.

Regards,

Debra Matteucci
Senior Editor & Editorial Coordinator
Harlequin Books
300 East 42nd Street
New York, New York 10017

THE BEWITCHING BACHELOR

CHARLOTTE MACLAY

Harlequin Books

TORONTO • NEW YORK • LONDON
AMSTERDAM • PARIS • SYDNEY • HAMBURG
STOCKHOLM • ATHENS • TOKYO • MILAN
MADRID • WARSAW • BUDAPEST • AUCKLAND

For Chuck, my own special Valentine and my favorite traveling companion. May the sun in our lives always outweigh the *stark bewölkt*.

ISBN 0-373-16620-6

THE BEWITCHING BACHELOR

Copyright © 1996 by Charlotte Lobb.

Printed in U.S.A.

Chapter One

Jet lag did strange things to a person.

Julianne Olson reached that conclusion as she peered through one barely open eye at the intruder in the bedroom she'd been assigned.

Granted her mother had weaned Julianne on Austrian folktales, but she'd never expected to wake up in her grandmother's castle on the edge of an alpine lake with a ghost entering the room through an oak armoire. The man in the short leather mountaineering pants that exposed his muscular thighs and rather adorable knees, looked like the perfect replica of a nineteenth-century daguerreotype, droopy mustache included.

She didn't feel particularly frightened, she realized as she considered the dreamlike quality of the experience. Indeed, she wasn't prone to nightmares and the only folktale that had ever troubled her was the one about a grumpy dragon who came out of his mountain cave every fifty years or so to steal a virgin from the nearby village.

With a sigh, she relaxed and let her eye close again. She doubted there'd be much interest among dragons these days in a twenty-six-year-old, unemployed virgin.

Something crashed.

With a start, Julianne bolted upright in bed. "What the devil are you doing?"

The ghost whirled, as though he hadn't been aware of her in the room, and his gray wig went slightly askew. "I am the one, *Fräulein,* who should be asking you that very same question." His accented English was rich with an imperious sounds of German. It wouldn't have mattered which of the two languages he'd spoken. Julianne had maintained her fluency in her mother's native language through both practice and study. It had been helpful in her work.

"I'm trying to get some sleep, that's what," she responded in English, since that had been his choice. "I had a horrendous flight, we were jammed elbow to elbow, not a vacant seat on the plane, and squalling kids the whole way. I nearly missed my connection and my body is telling me it's about 3:00 a.m. and I'm supposed to be in my deepest REM cycle." She brushed her hair back from her face in a weary gesture, only mildly curious about why a ghost would wear a wig. Or speak English. "So would you please go haunt someone else."

The corners of his lips twitched into the suggestion of a smile, making him appear much younger than his gray wig and mustache implied. Julianne got a seriously uncomfortable feeling that caused her skin to flush. Men, she realized, even ghostly apparitions, shouldn't be wandering around in her bedroom in the middle of the night.

"Haunt?" he echoed.

"That's what ghosts do, isn't it?"

"Oh, yes, that is one of the rules, I'm sure."

"Well, good..." She dragged the edge of the home-made quilt up to cover herself more modestly, not that her nightgown was all that see-through. It was simply the way the ghost was looking at her that made her uneasy. "Then, if you'll just be on your way..."

He tapped his heels together smartly and bowed. "As you wish, *Fräulein.*"

She made the mistake of closing her eyes. Briefly, she thought. And when she opened them, the ghost was gone. Vanished. Without a sound.

Hopping out of bed, she crossed the room in a hurry, the moonlight providing plenty of illumination in the unfamiliar room. She yanked open the armoire door.

Nobody there. Just a couple of garment bags her grandmother apparently used for storage and the few clothes that Julianne had had enough energy to hang before she'd collapsed into bed.

The back wall was cool to the touch and solid-sounding as she tapped on the wood. Only the odd scent of leather and spice lingered in the closet, a very masculine aroma.

With a shake of her head, she went back to bed. If only she'd been able to get a couple hours' sleep on the plane, her adjustment to the time change from Minnesota would have been so much easier. The tendency to experience hallucinations or, at the very least, bizarre dreams, was no doubt a part of jet lag.

She dreamed again later on, sometime in the dark of night when images eddy in uncertain currents, and the same man in his lederhosen costume appeared in the room. This time she had the distinct impression he had unpleasantly knobby knees.

Oddly, that was very reassuring.

SHE WOKE to full, glorious sunshine and a body that appeared ready to start the day. After dressing hurriedly in jeans and a cotton blouse, she took a moment to gaze out the window at the spectacular view that had been blurred by her fatigue when she'd arrived at Schloss Lohr—her grandmother's castle.

A narrow swath of silver blue touched the lakeshore opposite the castle, the land rising quickly beyond the water to fields of grass cut in an irregular checkerboard pattern in every imaginable shade of green. As the hills grew steeper, grass gave way to the deeper shades of forested slopes, spruce and pine and larch. Finally, above it all, the jagged peaks of the Alps, most topped with perpetual snow, rose into the cloudless sky.

Julianne grinned. If that view didn't drag a person right out of a blue funk—and glue together a broken heart—nothing would.

She tugged a comb through her short hair, then hurried down a narrow, twisting stairway with wooden steps worn smooth by thousands of treading feet. She looked forward to seeing her Grandmother Erna, and

Erna's niece Olga, who by some quirk of large families was so close in age to Erna that the two of them had been raised as though they were sisters. Indeed, everyone referred to Erna and Olga as "the Sisters."

"Ah, *Liebling,* my darling, you are up."

"Our little dumpling is awake."

The two aging women greeted Julianne enthusiastically. She kissed her bespectacled grandmother, a wisp of a woman with silver hair and mischievous gray eyes that sparkled behind thick lenses. "Thank you for letting me visit you, Grandma Erna."

"Go on with you, child. We are glad you finally came to visit two old, lonely women."

"You are the one who is *bony,* Erna," Olga announced loudly, wrapping her arms around Julianne in a hug worthy of the bears that used to roam the Alps. "I have enough meat on me for the two of us."

"I said *lonely,*" Erna shouted. "Turn up your hearing aid."

"Why would I want to *burn* my hearing aid? I spent good money for this device—"

Erna reached over and twisted the knob on the hearing aid. "Has the battery gone dead?"

Olga reared back. "You do not have to shout, sister. I can hear you just fine. We should be making our little Juli feel at home, not fussing at each other."

Rolling her eyes, Erna said, "We have coffee ready, *Liebling,* and some fresh bakery rolls. Come. Eat."

Julianne helped herself to coffee as black as dark molasses, added a good portion of milk and sugar to make it palatable, then settled into a straight-back chair at the kitchen table. The varnished pine wood shone with a fresh application of wax.

"So, how did you sleep, little dumpling?"

"Good dreams, we hope."

"Well, I..." Julianne's thoughts shifted to the image of the uninvited guest who had visited her bedroom during the night. She shrugged. "I guess the time change made me a little restless."

Olga patted her on the arm. "In a few days things will be better."

"You will sleep good in our mountain air." Erna bustled around the kitchen and presented Julianne with a small plate of cheese and sliced meat, along with a hard roll.

"I hope so. Last night I dreamed a ghost showed up in my room."

"Oh, how nice..."

"Frederick probably wanted to meet you."

Both sisters beamed a smile in her direction.

Julianne choked on her coffee. "Frederick?"

"Frederick Langlois. Such a nice man. He was hung, you know—"

"As a witch. Nearly a hundred and fifty years ago."

Frowning as she tried to make sense of the conversation, Julianne said, "I thought they did all that witch-burning business in the sixteenth century."

"Lohr am See has always been behind the times," Erna announced proudly. "Why, we didn't even have a regular doctor here in the village until long after I was born."

"Men are not witches, Erna," Olga admonished. "They are warlocks. I have told you that—"

"But Frederick says he is innocent—"

"Wait a minute," Julianne interjected, raising her hand like a traffic cop to halt the conversation. "Are you telling me there's a ghost in this castle?"

"Of course, dear." Still smiling, her eyes almost squinted closed behind thick lenses, Erna sat down across from Julianne and poured a helping of cream into her coffee cup.

"Everyone knows Schloss Lohr is haunted. Did not your dear mother tell you?"

Julianne shook her head, more to clear the cobwebs than to answer Olga's question. Obviously it took more than a single day to adjust to a transcontinental time change. On the other hand, she remembered her mother had been quite enamored of folklore, including ghost stories.

"Just what does your resident ghost look like?" she asked cautiously.

"Very handsome."

"Gray hair," Olga added. "And he has a charming mustache."

"A rather distinctive nose, wouldn't you agree, Olga? Aristocratic?"

"I have never noticed his *toes,* dear. He generally wears hiking boots, but he does have very spindly legs—for a man, you understand."

Julianne drank a large swallow of coffee, praying that the combination of bitter taste and a big dose of caffeine would set her equilibrium straight. By tomorrow, or surely the day after, she'd feel much more at home in this time zone and her brain wouldn't short-circuit at the least little thing.

"Do you, uh, see this ghost often?" Julianne asked. And is there a psychiatric hospital nearby? she wondered with some dismay. She hadn't been prepared to find the Sisters slipping into dementia.

"Indeed, he appears quite often."

"He can be quite pesky if we do something that upsets him."

"Upsets?"

"You know—leave the teapot on till the water boils away."

"Or forget to put the screen in front of the fireplace."

"He does get quite disturbed over very minor things. Rants and raves something terrible."

"His language can be quite shocking."

"He is a dear man. He cares, you know."

"I think you would call him a fussbudget."

Fussbudget? A ghost?

A niggling headache threatened at the back of Julianne's skull. She'd only meant to take advantage of exceptionally low airfares, visit her grandmother, and stoke the fires of her pride. She was darn proud of herself for having quit her job as a matter of principle when the boss had demonstrated his lack of trust in her abilities—the same boss with whom she'd thought she'd been in love. Thirty days of R and R. That's all she'd had in mind. Then she'd square her shoulders and rejoin the fray. Though she wasn't likely to risk her heart again soon.

Ghosts—and dementia—had not been on her vacation agenda.

"DID YOU DISCOVER anything last night?"

Erich Langlois rasped the hand file over a sharp edge of the crampon one more time before he looked up at his sister. "Not likely," he told her.

"But you did get into the castle?"

"Yes, the passageway was still there." He placed the crampon on his workbench among a clutter of other mountain climbing gear, right next to a gray wig and a ridiculously droopy fake mustache. "What I found, unfortunately, was a sleeping woman. An American, by the sound of her." A very attractive one with a shimmering halo of blond hair and wide, expressive eyes, but he wouldn't mention those small details to Helene.

"Did she see you?"

"She woke up when I stumbled over her suitcase, but I doubt she will remember much. With luck, she will believe I was nothing more than a dream. Or the ghost I was pretending to be."

"You will have to go back. We have to find some way to prove Schloss Lohr should never have been confiscated from our family and the name of Langlois stained with shame." Helene's lower lip formed a petulant pout and her eyes pooled with tears. At eighteen, there was still much of a child about her in spite of her height and the breadth of her shoulders. Her features were too prominent to be beautiful and a sulking look subtracted from even that marginal impression. "Erich, if you cannot clear our family name, Paul will not marry me. I cannot bear the thought—"

"Helene, I'll do the best I can, but I can't poke around the castle in the bright light of day. The Sisters would never allow it, and we have to move cautiously. Masquerading as the castle ghost seems the best way to proceed. Then, if the Sisters catch me, they'll be in a dither because they were visited by their ghost. Not that such a character actually exists, of course, but they're so balmy they think he does."

Wrapping his arms around his sister, Erich offered a reassuring hug as he had since they were children and he had shouldered much of the task of raising her. He knew how much she wanted to be accepted in the village, and her marriage to the son of the *Bürgermeister* would achieve that goal. Not that Paul Werndl would have been his choice for his sister.

Nevertheless, Erich had to do something.

The Langlois family had indeed lived as village outcasts for long enough. Erich had not minded the isolation or being targeted by bullies set on proving their bravery and making his life miserable. From the time he had been a young boy he had sought the solitude of the Alps for comfort. Now he had a thriving business as a guide for climbers willing to spend substantial amounts of money to safely reach the highest peaks in the region.

But Helene had found no such escape. She, like their mother, had suffered at the hands of superstitious villagers who continued to believe a Langlois capable of casting a curse that would bring illness to their children, or warts to their holier-than-thou noses.

It was time the truth was known. Frederick Langlois had no more been a witch than Erich was, and never should have been hanged, his property confiscated by the church and handed over to a conniving cousin, Egon Berker.

WALKING BACKWARD over the uneven cobblestones of the village square, Julianne gawked up at the church tower. Though it didn't compare to European cathedrals with their soaring spires, its very sturdiness seemed right for the tiny hamlet of Lohr am See. Solid. Able to endure harsh alpine winters with the same unyielding strength as the granite peaks surrounding the valley from which the dark stones had been quarried.

She snapped a picture with her automatic camera, turned and rammed into a wall just as solid as any mountain.

Her breath went whoosh and her head whipped up. Her startled gaze met two incredibly blue eyes hooded by dark brows that slanted downward in disapproval. At her shoulders she felt two strong hands steadying her... or preventing her escape. Her heart did a peculiar little somersault and she had the oddest feeling that the dragon had come down from the mountain to steal his virgin.

Her mind ordered her feet to run like hell, but her heart seemed to have another idea.

"Sorry..." She cleared her throat. "I wasn't watching where I was going."

"You appeared quite enthralled with our church," he replied in richly accented English.

"I am. It's lovely."

His eyes released their hold on hers and he shifted his attention to the church. "Architecturally, I have always felt it was a monstrosity. Nothing more than a box with a tower."

"Don't say that. It's perfect for the village. So... so enduring. I imagine you can see the tower from anywhere in the valley."

"Like the accusing finger of a parent determined to lay guilt on all of her children."

She stifled a laugh. "Well, *I* like it. My parents were married in the church and I've always wanted to visit the village."

The slightest twitch tilted the corners of his lips, and Julianne got the distinct impression that she had met this man before. Though that wasn't possible. She had only arrived at her grandmother's castle the previous evening.

"Would you like to see inside the church?" he asked.

"Is it open?"

"Always. They wouldn't want to miss an opportunity to welcome sinners."

"Are you?"

He frowned, confusion leveling his brows into a solid line. "Am I what?"

"A sinner?" Or, like the alpine myths, a dragon come down from the mountains?

In a studied perusal, his gaze swept with languorous ease across her face. "An unrepentant sinner, when the opportunity presents itself." His voice was low and raspy, unfairly intimate and deliciously accented, the quirk of his lips belying the arrogance of his words.

The forbidden thrill of danger curled through Julianne's midsection.

Cupping her elbow in a gesture that could only be described as possessive, he ushered her toward the heavy oak doors of the church. She caught the faint scent of his after-shave, leather and spice, and found the fragrance both enticing and familiar. Yet she couldn't quite recall what memory the aroma triggered.

Dressed in unrelenting black, the stranger wore a turtleneck sweater that tugged across his broad shoulders and slacks that hugged lean hips. He moved with surprising grace for a man of his size—well over six feet—and there didn't appear to be a spare ounce of fat on his lanky physique. Not exactly petite at five foot six, Julianne still had to hurry to keep up with his ground-swallowing strides.

"The church was built originally in 1502," he began as he pulled open the heavy door to the narthex. "It has burned at least twice and has been rebuilt virtually from the ground up."

Listening with one ear to his running commentary, Julianne drank in the somber elegance of the small chapel. She imagined her parents standing in front of the altar, beyond them, three vertical, stained-glass windows casting a rainbow of colors across the pews. In her mind she heard the whispered vows, pledges of eternal love she hoped would be hers one day to give and accept with a man of her own choosing. Only then would the empty feeling in her chest since her mother's death be made whole again.

She glanced up at the man who stood beside her.

Something shifted within her, stark and demanding, responsive to a chord as powerful as any played on a cathedral organ.

Swallowing hard, she asked, "Should I know you?"

"Probably not. I'm a simple mountain guide." He bowed slightly. "Erich Langlois."

The breath lodged in her lungs. "Are you related to—" She almost said, "The resident ghost of Schloss Lohr," then thought better of it. "Frederick Langlois?"

"My most infamous ancestor. A witch, they say, who tinkered with curses and assorted incantations." He leaned toward her, so close his breath was a wisp of warmth across her cheek, more imagined than felt. "The village gossips claim he could cause warts to grow on the end of a virgin's nose."

She sputtered, "Y-you're terrible!"

"And irreverent," he conceded. His lips slid into a smile that creased both of his cheeks, and Julianne knew, given the least little encouragement, her heart would be lost to this dark, dangerous man who had so easily cast a spell over her.

It was all she could do not to flee the church, and Erich Langlois, in a panic.

"WE REALLY MUST FIND time to take a drive up into the mountains while you are here," Erna said. "The views can be quite grand."

They'd all settled into a cozy parlor room after dinner where a small fire kept the evening chill at bay. Julianne found a spot at the end of the couch where she could curl up comfortably. Her eyelids were already heavy with fatigue and she wasn't sure how long she could manage idle chitchat with the Sisters.

"Did I ever tell you the story of how my sweet Josef once climbed to the highest peaks to bring me back a sprig of edelweiss?" Olga asked.

"Several hundred times," Erna mumbled under her breath, smiling tolerantly. "I was here, remember? You had sworn you would never marry Josef. Not in ten thousand years. Dreadful man, you said."

Olga giggled like a schoolgirl. "Ah, but that was before I knew how romantic he was."

To Julianne's surprise, the image of Erich Langlois popped into her mind. As dark and dangerous as he looked, she wondered if he could also be romantic. With a mental start, she dismissed the idea. She could hardly expect a man she'd only just met to drop by with a legendary bit of edelweiss, however intriguing he might otherwise be to her fanciful mind.

Julianne let her eyes close momentarily. She simply wasn't up to a conversation with the Sisters tonight. Nor did she want to dwell on thoughts of Erich Langlois.

"If you don't mind," she said, unfolding her legs and standing, "I'm going to have to call it a night. The time change—"

"We understand, *Liebling.*" Erna extended her hand to pull Julianne closer. "Give us a kiss, then off to bed with you."

"Don't let the bedbugs bite," Olga admonished, accepting her kiss in turn.

"I'll certainly try not to," Julianne agreed, remembering with a touch of nostalgia how her mother had always warned her of the same nighttime creatures. Though her mother had been dead now for three years, thoughts of her were never far from Julianne's mind, the grief still painfully new.

She climbed the stairs to her room, then hesitated in front of the closed door.

With a quick shake of her head, she assured herself there were no ghosts lurking inside. Fatigue had simply done strange things to her mind the prior evening—it had only been a dream, the Sisters' wild tale of ghosts to the contrary. The Alps were full of folklore, dragons and witches. Even a few imaginary bedbugs.

Slowly, she opened the door.

Moonlight spilled into the room, casting shadows that exaggerated the most innocent shapes—her nightgown draped over the back of a chair, the rounded lamp shade that could have been a head plucked from a hapless victim of the guillotine.

Quickly, she switched on the light. A sigh of relief escaped her lips as she stepped into the empty room and closed the door.

And then, quite suddenly, she wondered if she would ever draw another breath.

"Good evening, *Fräulein.*"

He was in her room. Again. The ghost. Short pants and bushy gray mustache included. Standing there with his arms crossed over a slightly paunchy stomach, his brows drawn in obvious displeasure. How on earth had her imagination conjured up adorable knees when his legs now appeared quite spindly? Or had the first visitation been nothing more than a dream?

"Was there..." The words squeaked. She cleared her throat and tried again. "Is there something I can do for you, sir?" Behind her, she searched for the doorknob. Perhaps she could escape. Call the police. Who did you call when you needed a ghost exterminator?

"You are a thoughtless girl."

"Me? Thoughtless?"

"You left your bed unmade this morning and the bathroom untidy. The Sisters are far too old and frail to follow around behind a healthy young woman like yourself and clean up after you."

Her gaze slid to the lovely four-poster bed, neatly made, the quilt folded with precision. "I didn't mean for them to have to—"

"*They* did not make your bed. *I* did. As I straightened the bath. And I do not intend to do so again when you are quite capable of such simple domestic tasks. My beloved Schloss Lohr has not yet fallen to the level of an inn for tourists."

"Yes, well, I'll certainly make my bed tomorrow and be careful in the bathroom. And every morning from now on."

"Even more serious," he continued in his chastising tone, "you left your curling iron plugged in. Are you not aware these newfangled electrical gadgets can start a fire?"

"I wasn't thinking—"

"Next time see that you do, *Fräulein*." He bowed slightly. *Arrogantly.* "Sleep well."

With that, he vanished. Poof.

He was there one instant and gone the next. No sound. The guy hadn't even bothered to walk through a solid wall. He'd simply disappeared. Or become invisible.

Her heart fluttering like a caged bird, and her knees going weak, Julianne sank to the edge of the bed.

Visiting her grandmother appeared to be filled with more surprises than she could have ever anticipated.

Had that strange man really been the ghost of Frederick Langlois? If so, who the devil had been the man with the far more impressive physique?

Shivering, Julianne wasn't sure she wanted to know the answer to either of those questions.

Chapter Two

The hinges on the old armoire squeaked. Erich winced and held his breath.

If there had been some other secret way into Schloss Lohr he would have taken it. Unfortunately, the passageway he had discovered as a child led only to this upstairs bedroom. Julianne Olson's bedroom. He had learned of the granddaughter's identity after asking a few questions in the village.

Cautiously, he stepped out of the armoire.

He had chosen the small hours of the morning for his second excursion into the castle in the hope that at this time of night Julianne would be sound asleep. That appeared to be the case. She was curled up on her side, her mouth slightly open, as though anticipating a kiss, her arms wrapped around a spare pillow. Sleep-mussed, silver blond curls brushed against her cheek.

With stern self-control, Erich quelled an uncharacteristic urge to slip into bed beside her and replace the pillow with himself.

It had been folly to banter with the American that afternoon. She might have recalled him from his previous visit. In fact, for a brief moment Erich thought he had detected recognition in her hazel eyes. But he had been so intrigued by the fresh innocence of her face, the way her nose tipped slightly, and her quick smile, he hadn't been able to help himself. Rarely did he indulge in flirtatious behavior with women. Today had been a mistake.

Now, as Julianne slept, she appeared utterly, completely guileless, and it was with considerable effort Erich reminded himself that her ancestors had stolen his birthright and had been the source of generations of Langlois misery.

As he slipped by her to the door into the hallway, she turned and muttered softly in her sleep. Her eyelids fluttered open, but her gaze remained blank and dream-filled.

"Rest well, Julianne Olson, descendant of the Berker clan," he whispered. "Such innocence as yours doesn't last long in this world."

He made his way downstairs to the library and began his laborious search for clues that would clear his family's name. Shortly before dawn he let himself out of the castle through the front door. It had been a frustrating night, reading detailed journal entries recorded more than a century ago. Frederick Langlois had been a consummate scholar and apparently nothing about the Lohr Valley and surrounding mountains had slipped his notice, very little of which appeared to have any significance for Erich's purposes.

If the journals had been kept chronologically, the search for clues might have been easier. As it was, each volume concentrated on a single topic—the local flora and fauna, crop yields, climatic changes, births and deaths in the village. It was impossible for Erich to know where he should begin looking. And, unless he was exceptionally lucky, the very last journal he read would be the one he'd been seeking all along.

As he hurried away from Schloss Lohr, he looked back over his shoulder. At a small window near the top of the signal tower, where the archbishop's men had once set beacons to warn of invaders, Erich thought he saw a movement. But that wasn't possible. The residents of the castle were still soundly sleeping. Or, at least, they should be.

THE ALPS were a wonderful place to walk.

Not that Julianne had attempted any strenuous mountain treks yet. Simply exploring the long, narrow valley with its winding paths and views of lushly green hillsides dotted with guernseys had been a balm to her spirits for the past three days.

She rose early every morning—straightening the sheet on her bed and folding the quilt almost as soon as her bare feet hit the plank floor. After coffee and rolls with the Sisters, she set off to visit a different part of the valley, eager to come upon a hillside covered with wildflowers in bloom, or to discover a farmhouse nestled in a secluded spot with pots of bright red geraniums decorating its window ledges.

Snatching up a blade of grass, she tucked the sweet-tasting tip in her mouth, and listened to the gentle call of cowbells across the hillsides. Maybe as an accompaniment to the bovine music she should take up yodeling, she mused with a smile.

She jumped over a rivulet of water that ran down toward the lake and continued to follow the path that led back to the highway and the village. It was almost lunchtime and the Sisters would be expecting her home.

Her footsteps slowed as she approached a house set well away from the road. Made of stone, it appeared isolated rather than secluded, as though the owners were not a welcome part of village life. The low stone wall that surrounded the house could have been intended to keep trespassers away or to imprison the occupants. Overgrown shrubbery nearly blocked the path to the front door.

The place wasn't abandoned, though.

At the side of the house, quite close to where Julianne would have to pass, a man dressed in blue mechanic's overalls was working under the hood of his car. Only lean hips and long legs were visible.

With the precision timing of a Swiss watch, he chose that instant to withdraw his head from the gaping engine compartment.

There was no mistaking Erich Langlois. His hair was as dark as a raven's wings, feathering at the nape of his neck, and his shoulders as broad as a fair-size mountain. He'd haunted Julianne's dreams for the past three nights, a swirling confusion of his ruggedly handsome face mingled with the visage of an aging, nagging ghost.

As he turned, Julianne knew she was trapped. She couldn't exactly skulk by without saying hello, nor could she in all good conscience flee back the way she had come. Although she was tempted. He did have the most unsettling effect on her.

She forced her brightest, the-customer-is-always-right smile. "Good morning, Erich. Lovely day, isn't it?"

His gaze swept over her with thoroughly masculine interest and she suddenly wished she were wearing a trench coat instead of shorts and a tank top. Or at the very least that she hadn't shed her light jacket and tied it around her waist.

"They say we will have rain by tomorrow."

"Oh, well, we'll just have to enjoy the sun while we can."

Wiping his hands on a greasy rag, he leaned back on the car's fender. "You like to hike?"

Remembering he was a mountain guide, she said, "I don't imagine I *hike* like you mean it. Walk, or stroll, is closer to the truth for my taste." She made a vague gesture that took in the surrounding mountains and all the wonderful craggy peaks. Wonderful craggy peaks to *look* at, she mentally added, not to go traveling across mountain-goat style, not with her serious case of acrophobia. Being anywhere higher than a stepladder terrified her. "Minnesota is pretty flat country compared to this."

"What do you do in Minnesota?"

"Did. I just quit my job." She felt her temper rising. The Marshall Hotel didn't deserve to have her as an employee, nor was Jerry Wiggins—the hotel manager—worthy of the love she'd considered offering.

Erich raised questioning brows.

"I was the reservations manager for a big hotel in Minneapolis," she explained. "There was this big convention scheduled. Two conventions, actually. Something went wrong. They probably shouldn't have been booked at the same time." She shrugged in an effort to ease the tension that was tugging at her shoulder blades. "Anyway, we ended up with two hundred overzealous plumbing contractors, who didn't have any rooms, trying to crash the lingerie distributors party. It was not a pretty sight."

He did it again, that little twitch of his lips that set Julianne's heart into overdrive.

"And you were blamed," he concluded.

"You'd think I had *scapegoat* stamped on my forehead in capital letters. The regional exec was having a fit and fingers were being pointed. The fact that the convention coordinator had blown the deal didn't matter. *She* was the one sleeping with the boss, not me. I walked out the minute I realized they were setting me up." The fact she'd actually been considering the possibility of sleeping with Jerry herself *really* ticked her off.

"You don't do that sort of thing?"

She bristled. No way was she going to confess that her heart had gotten involved and she'd actually been toying with the idea. "I work hard and I'm damn good at what I do. A woman shouldn't have to—" Realizing this conversation had become far too personal, she switched gears. "But you don't have any interest in my problems."

"On the contrary, Miss Olson, I find you more and more fascinating each time I see you. Perhaps even an obsession."

A surprising feeling of warmth curled through her midsection. "But we've only met once. In the village square."

"Yes, of course. I remember our meeting well." He shoved away from the car and carefully closed the hood. "Has a wart appeared on the end of your nose as yet?"

"Not that I've noticed."

"Ah, perhaps that means I've lost my powers of witchcraft."

Julianne doubted that was the case. He'd certainly cast a spell over her. She'd never felt so intrigued by a man, so drawn, or more aware of her own femininity. If she could have carried anything resembling a tune, she might have burst into song. But then she remembered that a vacation romance on the rebound wasn't part of her holiday package.

As it was, any melody she might have created stuck in her throat like a hacksaw blade when the back door to the house opened and a young woman of statuesque proportions stepped outside. One of Julianne's most inviolate rules was that she didn't mess with married men. Ever.

"I thought I heard voices," she said, eyeing Julianne with open curiosity.

"Come, meet our American visitor." Erich beckoned the young woman closer. "Julianne, may I present my sister, Helene."

A current of relief swept through Julianne as she noted Helene's youth and the close family resemblance between brother and sister. The girl had the same dark hair, strong features, and blue eyes, but on a woman they were a little overpowering. Julianne suspected, however, that with a bit of makeup and a more feminine hairdo, Erich's sister would be youthfully stunning.

"Julianne is staying with the Sisters at Schloss Lohr," Erich continued by way of further introduction.

Julianne smiled, genuinely pleased this woman was Erich's sister, not his wife. "I'm glad to meet you."

"You are a Berker." Helene made the name sound like the equivalent of some unpleasant rodent.

"My mother was a Berker. She married an American."

"I see." Helene's eyes narrowed. "How long do you plan to stay?"

Squirming under such intense scrutiny, Julianne said, "I have to use my return ticket within thirty days or it will cost me an arm and a leg to get back to the States." Which Julianne knew she couldn't afford, not when she was facing unemployment back home.

"Then I shall wish you a pleasant return journey back to America."

Julianne got the distinct impression that if she left for the airport that very minute it wouldn't be soon enough for Helene. And that was peculiar. In general, the villagers had gone out of their way to be friendly. Not Erich's sister, however. If anything, she radiated hostility. Or perhaps, in some misguided way, she was being protective of her big brother.

She slanted a glance at Erich. Come to think of it, he *would* make a heck of a souvenir of her visit to Austria.

The tapping of a horn from the nearby road saved Julianne from pursuing that thought any deeper, or from wondering further about Helene's animosity.

Grandmother Erna waved from the old Mercedes sedan. "Would you like a ride home, dear? We are just back from shopping."

"I'll be right there." Julianne let her farewell smile take in both Erich and his sister. "I'd better go."

He dipped his head in a gracious bow. "Until later, Juli*anna*." His quietly spoken words sounded like a promise, and the way he added the final syllable to her name, giving it the proper German pronunciation, settled around her like the warmth of a summer sun.

Once again Julianne got the impression she knew Erich from somewhere else, almost as though he'd always been a part of her dreams.

Idly wiping the grease from his hands, Erich watched as Julianne hurried to the waiting car. Slowly he returned his attention to his sister. "Was it necessary for you to be rude?"

"Why not? She is the heir to Schloss Lohr, Erich— the heir to what should rightfully be ours."

"She's not responsible for the past deeds of others. She at least deserves common courtesy."

Helene's eyes widened and she cocked her head to the side. "*Ach, ja,* now I see how it is," she teased. "You are attracted to this American woman."

"That, little sister, is no concern of yours." Helene had struck far too close to the truth. He didn't want her to know how much he looked forward to slipping into Julianne's bedroom each night. In spite of his best efforts to keep his thoughts on the search for clues, he had become an all-too-eager voyeur. Such a weakness in self-control did him no credit. He was well aware that a liaison with the heir to Schloss Lohr was quite impossible when he was trying to wrest the inheritance from her grasp.

"Perhaps if you are unable to prove our ancestor was hung in error, you could pursue the American," Helene said, pure devilment in her eyes. "Your marriage to her would assure we Langlois would once again control both the castle and the surrounding land with all the tenant farmers."

He scowled at his sister. "You go too far, Helene. I have no intention of marrying any woman simply to gain control of an estate, large or small. Indeed, I question that Paul Werndl truly loves you if he contin- ues to insist our name be cleared before he offers marriage. He would ignore the curse of witchcraft if he really cared for you.''

The panic of denial drained Helene's face of color. ''It is because of his job. A banker has to be above reproach. He's told me that's the only reason he cares about that old witch story at all.'' Her chin quivered. ''He loves me, I know he does.''

''It's all right, Helene. I will find a way to clear our name. I promise.'' Sighing, he gave her a smile he hoped was encouraging. She was so young, too young to be considering marriage. But Erich had never been able to deny his sister her smallest wish if it was within his power to grant. Not since their mother had deserted the family so many years ago. ''Now, since I have your car back in working order, would you consider fixing my lunch?''

She readily agreed, giving him a sisterly kiss of appreciation before returning to the house.

Erich remained troubled, however. He doubted that Julianne would think his motivation for disinheriting her particularly noble. But an error had been made in the past and needed correcting.

''DID YOU HAVE a nice visit with the Langlois?'' Erna asked. She drove with a heavy foot on the accelerator, a troubling habit in Julianne's view, given her grandmother's poor eyesight and the narrow roadway to the castle.

She gripped the armrest in the back seat. ''I just happened on Erich when he was working on his car.''

"I did not know he worked at a *bar*," Olga said. She appeared quite calm in spite of the way Erna drove. Maybe her vision could use testing, too, along with a new set of batteries for her hearing aid.

"A nice boy," Erna conceded.

"Handsome," Olga remarked. "But I thought he worked as a guide, not in a bar."

"I said *car*, Olga, not *bar*." Julianne made it a point to raise her voice a little louder to be heard over the sounds of the vehicle. "I met his sister."

Olga fussed with her hearing aid. "Poor little Helene. She has never had many friends."

"But remember, dear, it has always been difficult for the Langlois in our village. Perhaps it is not her fault she stays so much to herself."

"Their mother went quite mad," Olga said. "It was rumored their father had cursed her, but naturally we did not believe such a wild tale."

"It was a tragedy, that is what is was." Erna brought the car to a jarring halt as if to emphasize the point. "Erich was only a lad at the time, a rather gangly boy."

"All arms and legs, as I recall."

"He seems to have grown into them nicely," Julianne murmured out loud, recalling with considerable pleasure the breadth of his shoulders.

The Sisters giggled, the sound as youthful as if they were still twenty and discussing a young man in the village who had caught their eye.

Smiling, Julianne carried the net shopping bag into the kitchen for the Sisters and set it on the counter. A long loaf of bread jutted out the top, along with a matching roll of sausage. She started putting things away while Erna and Olga wandered off to hang up their wraps.

It was some time before Erna returned.

"I get so angry with myself!" she complained.

"What's wrong, Grandmother?"

"Ach, I took off my glasses to wash my face and now I cannot seem to remember where I left them." She squinted around the kitchen counter. "Do you see them, dear? I cannot imagine where I put them."

Julianne followed Erna's gaze, though she suspected her grandmother had left her glasses in plain sight in the bathroom, or maybe her bedroom. Turning, she said, "I'll go look—"

She was going mad. Absolutely mad. Or else her own eyesight had gone on the fritz.

A pair of glasses floated into the kitchen. In midair. With complete precision, they landed on the table without so much as a whisper of sound.

Julianne swallowed hard. "Grandmother?"

"Yes, dear."

"Your glasses—I think they're on the table."

"Really? How silly of me. Why would I have left them there?"

Julianne didn't know why. Nor could she explain how glasses floated with ease through the air. She did know her right eye had developed an irritating tic, and a headache was threatening at her temple.

She did not—absolutely *not*—believe in ghosts. Not benevolent phantoms who made beds and delivered misplaced glasses. At least, she hadn't believed in ghosts until she arrived at Schloss Lohr.

HOW MUCH COURAGE should it take to walk into your own bedroom?

Not much, Julianne decided that evening, squaring her shoulders. Ghosts were only figments of an over-active imagination, she assured herself. And if they weren't, she was going to find out why.

Cautiously she twisted the door handle and peeked inside.

"There, what did I tell you?" she said out loud, smiling at her small victory. The room was empty. Jet lag was a thing of the past.

With newly found valor, she examined the armoire in detail. Made of dark oak, it seemed solid enough. Once she shoved her clothes and a few items that had been stored there aside, there was certainly enough room to stand, although a tall man might have to duck.

She ran her fingers along every seam in the back wall looking for the telltale sign of a doorway or a switch that would reveal a secret passage. Nothing. She could have been in her own apartment in Minneapolis for all the hidden doors she found.

Still, she'd had so many troubling dreams since she'd arrived at the castle—all of them related to the ghost of Frederick Langlois—and so many daytime thoughts about the intriguing Langlois descendant, she was determined to discover the source of her restless feelings.

If the ghost she'd seen—or imagined—was more corporeal than spirit, with a few magic tricks up his sleeve, she needed to find out. For all she knew, some homeless guy had taken up residence in the castle without the Sisters' permission. In Minneapolis that would be a potentially dangerous situation.

So she set a trap.

From her travel sewing kit, she took a long piece of black thread and tied it to the handle of the armoire, which opened toward the far wall from the bed. She readied herself for the night, then tied the opposite end of the thread around her wrist. She reasoned that if the armoire door opened it would tug hard enough to wake her but not enough to alert the intruder. And a human trying to walk past her would break the thread without being any the wiser. A ghost, she assumed, wouldn't budge the thread at all.

Lord, she was muddled, totally unsure who or what she was trying to trap.

For a long time she tried to stay awake, thinking that was an even better way to catch whoever had been her nightly visitor. Eventually, however, her eyelids grew heavy, the silver cast of the waning moon no match for a day spent hiking through the hills. She rolled onto her side, pillowing her head on her hand.

WHEN THE TUG CAME her hand flopped away from her head. Startled awake, Julianne almost cried out before she remembered the trap she'd laid.

Her heart raced. Through slitted eyes she watched a man step out of the armoire. He wore the familiar lederhosen, and as he paused beside her bed—overly long, she thought as she struggled not to give away the fact she was awake—she noted his muscular thighs. He was definitely in great shape for a ghost. Decidedly solid, and not at all like the ghost who had instructed her on her housekeeping duties.

She could have confronted him right there in the bedroom, but curiosity compelled her to discover what the ghost of Schloss Lohr was up to. If she could.

He moved silently and with considerable grace toward the door. Perhaps old ghosts weren't troubled by the aches and pains of human ailments like arthritis. Though as she thought about it, the nagging phantom who'd been so concerned about her curling iron starting a fire had seemed a bit stooped.

An instant later, her visitor opened the door and stepped into the dark hallway. He hadn't walked *through* the door as Julianne imagined a ghost might. In fact, he'd behaved in quite a *human* way—a little too human when she considered just how long he had gazed down at her in bed.

She leapt to her feet, found her robe and slippers, and with all the stealth she could muster, followed him out the door. From the top of the stairs she saw the glow of a flashlight disappear into the library.

You'd think a ghost who'd been living in the castle for a hundred and fifty years would know his way around well enough not to need a light.

Wishing she had been as smart as the ghost about carrying a flashlight, she made her way to the library. She could see a crack of light beneath the door and hear movement in the room. With her hand on the knob, she hesitated. According to the Sisters, their ghost was thoroughly benevolent. But if the man she'd been following wasn't really a ghost....

Belatedly, she looked around for a weapon.

The layout of the first floor featured a long hallway with rooms to either side. It would have been a great place to practice bowling—or a wonderfully well-arranged small hotel, perhaps a bed and breakfast—except Julianne had other matters on her mind at the moment. Every few feet along the hallway, a straight-back chair had been placed against the wall, or a table topped with a vase full of flowers, to break the monotony of the corridor. Decorations were sparse.

Then she remembered the crossed swords mounted on the wall, souvenirs of two Berker brothers who had served in World War I. Feeling her way in the darkness, she stood on a chair and retrieved one of the swords. It felt heavy in her hand, and dangerous.

At the library, she took a deep breath and pulled open the door.

"Stay right where you are, mister!" She brandished the sword at the man behind the big oak desk, his face shadowed by the lamp shade.

Slowly he stood—big and tall and decidedly familiar.

"If you are planning a duel, Juli*anna*, I trust you will provide me with a suitable weapon. I seem to have left mine at home."

"Erich?" The word caught in her throat and the tip of her sword quivered.

Chapter Three

Erich pulled the wig from his head and tossed it onto the desk, then did the same with the fake mustache. He'd never been challenged by such a spirited woman, and certainly never by one with a sword in her hand.

To disguise the amused smile that threatened, he bowed slightly. "I'm sorry you have discovered me."

"I just bet you are! What the devil are you doing in my grandmother's castle in the middle of the night anyway?"

He kept a wary eye on the circling tip of the sword. Americans, as he had learned leading a good many mountain climbing expeditions with them, could be unpredictable. "Would you believe insomnia?"

"Not likely." She crossed the room, the sword held at a threatening angle, her expression filled with righteous indignation.

Had the circumstances been different, Erich would have found her attitude endearing. Now, however, he knew he had to tread with caution. Julianne was, after all, a Berker by birth, and therefore not entirely trustworthy.

He closed the handwritten journal he'd been reading and placed it with the others at the side of the desk. "Perhaps you would believe I am investigating the untimely demise of my great-great-grandfather—several times removed—Frederick Langlois."

"And to do that you found it necessary to masquerade as his ghost?"

"At the time it seemed a clever idea. Now that I have been found out..." He shrugged. Indeed, Julianne's interference did require him to develop a new plan of attack.

"You've been sneaking into my room, haven't you? Every night!" Her face flushed a charming shade of crimson, either from anger or embarrassment at having been observed while sleeping, Erich surmised.

"A harmless endeavor, I assure you." Except for a few wayward thoughts, he'd had no intention of taking advantage of the situation. "There is a hidden passageway from the garden to your room. I suspect there was once a chatelaine of the castle who enjoyed clandestine adventures of an amorous nature."

"Just because you knew of the passageway, did you think you had a right to come sneaking in here? If you wanted to read those books—" she tapped the top journal with the tip of her sword "—why didn't you simply ask the Sisters?"

"I doubt they would appreciate my prying." Nor the reason for his search.

"Well, they certainly wouldn't appreciate you sneaking around the place like some criminal. My gosh, Erich, if I'd had a gun I might have shot you."

His brows rose in mock surprise. "I would not have thought you such a violent person."

She glared at him, though since she was dressed in a modest blue-flowered nightgown and robe, she appeared more vulnerable than fierce.

"Don't press your luck," she insisted. "You're trespassing, and where I come from that's a crime." Flicking the blade toward the door, she said, "I think you'd better get out of here while you can. And trust me, you'll need a battering ram to get through the door of the armoire next time."

Erich raised his hands in a show of compliance and stepped around the desk. Julianne would be easy enough to disarm. He doubted she had ever used a sword, but at the moment he had other matters on his mind. If he was no longer free to search the castle he might never clear the Langlois name. A great deal rested on his success, including his sister's happiness. Perhaps if he played on Julianne's sympathies he could gain her cooperation.

"Are you familiar with the history of Schloss Lohr?" he asked.

"I know Frederick Langlois was hanged as a witch."

"Did you also know that at the same time three women were burned at the stake for delving into witchcraft?" The shake of Julianne's head told him that part of the story had not been passed on to the current heir to the castle. "Frederick's wife, who was pregnant, and his five-year-old son were banned from the castle after the hanging, and all of his property was confiscated."

Her lovely hazel eyes clouded with just the sympathy Erich was hoping for. "That's terrible," she said. "I've never understood how anyone could believe in witches. In this day and age it seems so unjust."

"More than that. His wife, Kathe, was much younger than Frederick and was never suspected of witchcraft herself. She was, however, sentenced to be placed in stocks. Because she could not feed or care for herself, her son—a child—had to beg in the streets for food. The villagers were only generous enough that she and the boy stayed alive . . . barely." Through a thousand retellings, the story of his family's martyrdom had been burned into Erich's memory as painfully as if he and his sister had suffered the same indignities. Indeed, with only minor variations on the theme, the burden had been carried by each new generation of the Langlois family. In earlier generations, women had been stoned. Now the villagers limited themselves to hurling verbal abuse, crossing themselves and stepping out of the way as a Langlois walked past.

"But why would someone falsely accuse Frederick of being a witch?" Julianne asked.

"Greed, of course. His cousin, Egon Berker, had made a political alliance with the archbishop. Berker wanted the castle and all of the lands for himself. He sacrificed Frederick for the good of his purse."

"Are you saying my ancestor lied in order to gain control of the property?"

"Absolutely. I also suspect he wanted Frederick's young wife and hoped to get her in the bargain." As he had been telling the tale, Erich had moved closer to Julianne, close enough so he could see the golden specks of reflected light in her eyes. "And now it is past time that the wrongs done to Frederick Langlois be righted." With a movement so subtle that he caught her off guard, Erich disarmed Julianne.

She gasped as he pulled her slender body up tight against his.

Instantly he regretted his ill-considered action. She felt far too good in his arms, as though she had been especially created to fit within his embrace. Through the light fabric of her gown he could feel her pert breasts pressing against his chest. The pleasing sensation set up an instant and unwelcome reaction in his groin. She was, after all, the enemy—a Berker.

He eased his hold on her and schooled his features not to give away the jolt of need he had felt, not only a physical need but the craving for some emotion far deeper that had always eluded him. He had finely honed the ability to hide his feelings in the same way he had developed his skill at scaling vertical walls high in the Alps. For Erich, the mastery of both talents was necessary for survival.

"I need your help, Julianna," he whispered, his voice thickening on her name with unintended intimacy. "I need you to help me set things right."

Julianne figured she was going to have to learn how to breathe all over again. She was drowning in the blue pools of Erich's eyes, so dark they were almost black, depthless and dangerous. Her hands palmed his rock-solid chest and her fingers flexed into the sturdy cotton fabric of his shirt. Although he had eased his grip, they were still standing too close, his rich scent of leather and spice surrounding her as surely as his arms. She sensed that against Erich she'd be defenseless, with or without the sword.

"Help?" she repeated.

"I've found Frederick's journals. He was a meticulous man who recorded his life in considerable detail. Somewhere in those weighty tomes is the evidence I need to prove he was unjustly accused."

Julianne let her gaze sweep across the bound volumes on the desk, then circle the walls of books that filled the library. There were two entire shelves of journals just like those Erich had been studying, a lifetime's worth of notes. It would take him months to read every entry.

"What will you do if you find what you're looking for?" she asked.

"I will petition the magistrate to return Schloss Lohr to its rightful owners."

Anxiety prickled along the back of Julianne's neck. "Grandmother Erna is the owner of the castle. She's lived here all of her adult life. My mother was born here."

His silence filled the room so completely it began to press in on Julianne's ears. She could hear her blood pulsing through her heart like a steady drumbeat. Her eyes widened as realization filled her head with silent fury. "You want the castle for yourself! You're not nobly trying to right any ancient wrong, you're trying steal the castle from my grandmother!"

"The Langlois continue to suffer because of Egon Berker's greed."

Shocked and hurt, she took a step back, away from Erich and his tantalizing scent. "Maybe you'd like to put Erna in stocks for a while. Would that even the score?"

"You don't understand."

"You can bet your cute little leather britches, I understand perfectly. Greed is a universal language that's never needed any translation." She waved her hand in the direction of the door. "I want you out of here right this minute or I'll call the cops and have you arrested for trespassing."

His brows lowered with an anger that matched her own. "I *will* clear the Langlois name."

"Not with my help," she vowed.

As he headed for the door she added, "And you can mind your own damn business about whether or not I make my bed in the mornings."

Turning, he slanted her a puzzled look. "I assure you, *Fräulein,* your domestic habits are no concern of mine and never have been."

"Oh, no?" She hooked the back of her wrist on her hip. "Then tell me, if it wasn't you nagging me, who was it?"

"I haven't the vaguest notion."

With that he exited the room, leaving Julianne with the memory of his cute buns, well-muscled legs covered in dark hair, and a niggling headache threatening at her temples.

She closed her eyes, recalling another man with spindly legs and a tummy that in no way matched Erich's well-developed physique. If Erich hadn't been the ghost who had ordered her to shape up her housekeeping act, then who had? Surely there weren't two impostors roaming the halls of Schloss Lohr. For her own sanity—and in spite of what the Sisters had said—she didn't want to consider the possibility that there really was a ghost in the castle.

JULIANNE EXAMINED a bouquet of spring flowers as the animated conversation of the villagers flowed around her.

Market day in Lohr am See was a bustling social occasion. Farmers from miles away arrived early to set up stands displaying their produce in the village square. Bright red strawberries vied for space with heads of butter lettuce and luscious baked goods made by the farmers' wives. Off to one side a group of itinerant Basque musicians from Spain played a lively tune in the hope that a few coins would be tossed into the open violin case that lay on the cobblestones in front of them.

Housewives from the village filled their shopping baskets with fruit and vegetables while catching up on the news of their neighbors.

Fascinated, Julianne tagged along beside Erna and Olga as they examined each head of lettuce or roll of sausage as though inspecting the crown jewels for possible flaws.

"These oranges cannot be from around here," Olga said, lifting one and sniffing it.

"They are from Israel," Erna told her.

"Of course they are *real,*" Olga agreed, "but they were not raised anywhere in Austria unless it was in a hothouse." She replaced the orange on the vendor's display, shaking her head as though the man had violated some crucial law of nature.

Julianne grinned. The Sisters were quite the pair.

"Juli, dear, would you do us a favor," Erna whispered conspiratorially.

"Of course, Grandma. Whatever you want."

"There is a woman down the way selling little animal decorations made of cookie dough. They are not terribly clever, but would you mind buying one or two?"

"I'd be happy to, but—"

"Gerta is the wife of one of our tenant farmers. A dear lady, truly she is. But they have had such a dreadful time lately making ends meet, as have many of the villagers. So many imports now compete with what they can produce."

Understanding the purchase would be as much charity as commercial, while still providing a way for the woman to save face, Julianne nodded. "I need to start buying a few souvenirs," she assured her grandmother. "What better choice than something that's been made right here in Lohr am See?" Among the people Julianne's mother had once known and loved.

Going off by herself, she made her purchases—a cookie kitten with a lopsided grin and a little gray mouse with a curling tail. Her biggest reward was the way Gerta was so visibly pleased by the few Austrian schillings she had earned. It seemed like such a small thing, and Julianne wondered if there were other ways she could help the local economy.

Quite content with the value she'd received with her purchases, Julianne thanked the farmer's wife and turned away.

Her smile faded, however, and her stomach tightened when she spotted Erich and his sister shopping on the opposite side of the square. She hadn't seen him since she'd caught him in the library two days ago. And with her armoire door barricaded, she'd had no middle-of-the-night visitors.

Still, a niggling sense of guilt for not helping Erich had been teasing at the back of her mind. It wasn't her fault that some long-buried ancestor hadn't been entirely honest, she told herself. Everybody had a horse thief or two in their backgrounds and no one expected them to make reparations to the injured parties. Why should her grandmother be the one to pay the price?

As she headed for the Sisters, who had moved on to another vegetable stand, Julianne found herself surreptitiously tracking Erich's movements. Too bad his nefarious scheme to dislodge Erna from the castle had nipped the budding attraction she'd felt for the darkly handsome man.

She sighed, figuring he hadn't returned her feelings anyway. Nor did she need to get involved in a vacation romance that had no hope for the future. Unfortunately, none of that stopped her from admiring the way his cable-knit sweater tugged across his shoulders and stretched to circle his muscular forearms.

Clearly, she didn't have a real good track record when it came to her choice in men. Apparently she had a knack for being attracted to men who simply wanted to use her to make them look good. She wasn't about to take the plunge again anytime soon.

From an alley between buildings a motor scooter raced into the square, its two-cylinder engine popping, the sound echoing off the stone masonry. The driver was a boy of about fourteen who appeared set on using pedestrians as pylons in an obstacle course. Housewives leapt out of his path, shopping bags flying from their hands. Children screamed. Showing off to a gaggle of teenage girls, the driver wove his way past the musicians, then turned sharply in front of a stall loaded with lettuce and onions.

His front tire hit a puddle of water that covered the rough cobblestones and the scooter went out of control, careening crazily. As though in slow motion, the scooter fell to its side, throwing its rider, and continued its forward motion in a lopsided slide that took it right into the vegetable stand. Wood cracked and shattered. Lettuce exploded into the air and a barrage of onions bombarded nearby shoppers.

Erich and his sister were among those who scattered to avoid injury.

The vendor cursed and shook his fist at the boy.

To Julianne's surprise, the kid bounced to his feet, apparently unharmed, shouting, "It was not my fault!" He pointed an accusing finger at Helene Langlois. In rapid-fire German, he added, "She did it! The witch. It was her evil eye that made me lose my balance."

The poor girl blanched and her hand flew to her mouth.

Shocked silence sliced with a biting edge across the square. Onlookers stood motionless, their mouths open, as if by moving a single muscle they might bring down the witch's curse on their own heads.

Into that void, Erich stepped protectively in front of his sister. The outrage he felt was like a gathering storm, dark and threatening. He balled his hands into frustrated fists. Would the villagers never forget the Langlois shame? Would the cruel taunts never cease?

"You are the devil's own whelp, Peter Aberer, and all of these people know it. You have no license to drive that scooter and even less sense."

The boy took a step back, his eyes wide even as he continued his defiance. "It is true. My pa told me—"

"Your father ought to spend more time applying a stick to your backside instead of spreading old wives' tales." Erich righted the motor scooter. The front wheel was bent and the fender badly scraped. It was fortunate for the youngster he had not been seriously injured. "Your father is not going to be pleased at the damage you have done and how much he will have to pay this farmer."

"He owes nothing. It is the witch—"

Erich fisted the boy's shirt. He was only a child, he reminded himself, a child repeating tales he had heard from his elders.

Tamping down the useless fury that knotted in his gut, Erich released the boy. He'd leave the youngster for the farmer to deal with.

As he turned away, Erich saw Julianne in the crowd, a witness to the telling incident. Their eyes locked for an instant, hers shocked and sympathetic, his still filled with anger. Now she would know how it had always been for the Langlois and he wondered if she would reconsider her decision about righting the terrible wrongs her ancestor had set in motion. But it was not her pity he wanted. Only justice.

"Leave the American woman alone," Helene pleaded in his ear. "We have no use for her. She is a Berker."

One hundred and fifty years of Langlois pride warred with his need to end the family's bondage to a lie. "We could use her help."

"We need no one, Erich. Only the two of us, as it has always been. She will be leaving Schloss Lohr soon enough and then you can continue your search." She tugged on his arm. "Come home with me."

He glanced around the square. The villagers were going back to their own business and someone had found Peter's father to deal with the farmer.

"You go ahead," Erich said, quelling her further objections. "There is something I want to do."

A path opened in front of Erich as he walked across the square, the villagers avoiding him as though he might be a carrier of some ancient plague. He ignored the way their eyes darted anxiously in his direction as he passed. Only in some festering spot in his soul did the pain of ostracism continue its raw throb, like a wound that never quite healed.

JULIANNE SAW HIM coming. Erich looked the part of a fierce dragon with his dark brows drawn downward, his well-sculpted lips pulled into a grim line. His anger was so palpable, she wouldn't have been surprised to see him breathe fire. Nor would she have blamed him.

The Sisters had wandered off to continue their shopping and Julianne greeted Erich with a simple, "I'm sorry."

"Apologies gain little for the Langlois."

"No one except you even stepped forward to defend your sister, much less point out that boy had been driving recklessly and the accident was entirely his fault."

"They never do. Not when my sister is involved."

"Why on earth doesn't she move away from Lohr am See? It has to be terrible for her living here in the valley. For both of you."

"Perhaps we are a stubborn pair."

Determined, too, Julianne suspected, and she'd always been a sucker for the underdog. "I know the way the villagers treat you is blatantly unfair, and it goes against everything I believe in, but you surely can't expect me to help you evict my grandmother from Schloss Lohr."

"We are not discussing eviction, Julianna. We are talking about the truth. Can you turn your back on justice here in Austria when you were quick to defend yourself from those in America who had sought to blame you unfairly?"

The man really knew how to push her buttons. Over the years Julianne had marched and carried picket signs for a half dozen causes she considered just—higher wages for teachers, more and better shelters for battered women, advocacy for victims' rights. She was a flaming liberal, she admitted. Seeing how Erich and his sister were treated by the villagers galled the heck out of her. She wanted to *do* something to make amends, to fight for the underdog.

Unfortunately, carrying a picket sign didn't appear to be the solution to Erich's problem.

"I simply can't go behind my grandmother's back to search—"

"Then help me convince the Sisters that I should have a right to read my ancestor's journals. That's all I am asking."

"And if the journals don't reveal what you're hoping they will?"

"I will deal with that later."

And very likely draw Julianne more deeply into taking part in separating Erna from her beloved castle. "I don't know..."

"Even if I found evidence of Frederick's innocence, there is no assurance the government would act on that information and restore Schloss Lohr to my family. But I would be able to clear the Langlois name."

"It's that important to you?"

"It is to my sister. The man she loves will not marry her until the stain has been removed from our name."

She raised her brows in surprise. "You're kidding."

"It's not something I'd joke about."

Julianne conceded that was no doubt the case. In fact, she wished Erich had more reason to smile. His grim determination made her want to lighten his burdens so she could see his cheeks crease with that devastating smile of his, a truly selfish desire, she realized, when he was motivated by the far nobler need to defend his sister. She was always impressed by siblings who were loyal to each other and she found herself admiring that attribute in Erich. And Helene, of course, she added as a none-too-kind afterthought.

As she looked into Erich's startlingly blue eyes, she realized he had stepped closer. Almost too close. He raised his hand and with his fingertip he brushed back a flyaway curl from her face. His touch was feather-light—seductively so.

"I understood Americans believed in justice above all else," he said in a low whisper that swept through her as electricity flows through an uninsulated wire, hot and dangerous.

She swallowed hard. "It was a basic tenet of our forefathers, I suppose." At the moment she wouldn't have been able to name a single signer of the Declaration of Independence, or even tell him who had been the first president. Her mind was a blank, but other parts of her anatomy had definitely revved up to full speed. Her heart rate had accelerated and her breathing was labored. Somewhere low in her body she felt an unfamiliar throbbing sensation.

"Then you will help me gain access to Frederick's journals?"

Lord, it would take a will of steel to deny this man anything. He was deliberately, skillfully, seducing her with his voice, his eyes, his touch. And Julianne's resistance appeared to be at a low ebb. She nodded her agreement.

Her reward was a half smile that canted his lips and did something warm and wonderful to her insides.

A bell began to strike a heavy, metallic sound and it took her three strokes of the clapper before she realized the ringing wasn't coming from inside her head but from the church tower bell announcing midday. With difficulty, she pried her gaze from the hypnotic pull of

Erich's eyes. Only then was she able to draw a steady breath.

The village square seemed filled with renewed activity, people shuffling around and changing positions. Then from out of a stone building adjacent to the church a creature the likes of which Julianne had never seen appeared.

The square filled with gasps and rippled applause.

Hidden by a horrific wooden mask with horns and a red-painted mouth, the creature danced in lumbering steps around the square. He was dressed all in black and a cowbell hung from his waist, clanking at each step. Arms waving, he chased after giggling children and made low, threatening sounds at the ladies.

"Who or what on earth is that?" Julianne asked, laughing at his antics.

"That is Hans, the curator of our small village museum. He likes to dress up as Krampas, the mythical goblin of the Alps, and show off his costume on market days. Originally Krampas only appeared on December fifth to frighten children who had been bad, a precursor to old St. Nick, I am told. But Hans thinks his appearance stirs up business for his museum."

"Or scares it away," she observed with another laugh.

The costumed Krampas danced his way over to Julianne. He made low, grunting noises as he hopped from foot to foot, but behind the mask, brown eyes twinkled with mirth.

"I promise I'll be good from now on," Julianne assured him.

He brought her hand to his wooden lips, offering a gallant kiss.

Then, for one brief moment, the eyes behind the mask darted a glance toward Erich that could only be described as malevolent. Before Julianne could be sure what she'd seen, the costumed character danced off to harass other onlookers.

"What was that all about?" Julianne asked.

"Hans has some very strong views about who should be allowed to reside in his village."

Julianne was still pondering Erich's strange response when Erna and Olga joined them.

"Are you ready to go, dear?" Erna asked. "I think we have purchased all we need for today."

"We are going to bake you a strawberry torte," Olga announced, beaming with pride. "It is my own special recipe."

"In the entire village, Olga is the best cook," Erna said.

"The recipe is not in a *book,* dear, it is in my head. I learned it from my mother."

Smiling, Julianne said, "I'm sure the torte will be delicious." She glanced at Erich and felt the persuasive power of his personality. "Grandmother, there's something Erich would like to talk to you about. It's rather serious."

Behind her thick lenses, Erna blinked rapidly. "In that case, dear boy, you must come to supper. You can share in Olga's torte and we will have a nice, long conversation.''

"I would be honored, Frau Berker."

Erich bowed his head in acknowledgment of the invitation but his eyes didn't leave Julianne's. Although she had provided the opening, she wondered if her grandmother had just made a serious mistake in judgment by inviting the dragon into her home.

"IS IT NOT THRILLING?"

"Of course the icing is not *chilling,* dear. It would be far too difficult to spread that way." Olga plucked a stem from a juicy red strawberry and dropped the fruit into a bowl.

"No, I meant it is *thrilling* that Erich Langlois is coming to supper. He is such a handsome young man and they make such an attractive couple."

"Which couple is that, dear?"

"Erich and our Juli, of course!" In exasperation, Erna added a second teaspoon of sugar to her coffee and stirred vigorously. "Can you not see how nice the two of them look together, him so dark and our Juli so fair like her mother? They would have such lovely children."

Cocking her head to one side, Olga gazed suspiciously at her aunt. "You are up to mischief again, I know it."

Erna's cheeks flamed with a blush. "Surely you would agree it would be nice to see those two young people get together and fall in love. Then our Juli would live nearby.''

"Young people these days do not appreciate old ladies meddling in their affairs." The warning came with a smile almost as mischievous as that of her aunt's.

"Then we must be very careful not to let them know what we are up to."

Olga's giggle began with a series of quick little hiccupping sounds. Erna tittered a quarter octave higher. Soon they were trying desperately to suppress a frenzy of giggles so Julianne would not come from the parlor to investigate what was going on in the kitchen.

"I do...believe," Olga said between gasping breaths, "we will be even more successful...than when we matched Konrad Fessenger with his sweet little wife, Maria. They have been so happy together."

"Oh, yes, dear sister, this will be a wonderful match." Erna gave her sister-in-mischief a delighted, conspiratorial hug.

Chapter Four

"Oh, my..." Erna gasped.

From the corner of his eye, Erich caught sight of Erna bringing the soup tureen to the table. Unbalanced, she tripped then righted herself as the porcelain bowl, instead of spilling its contents, settled gently on the polished rosewood tabletop. At least that's what he thought he'd seen. In truth, he'd been far more engaged in observing Julianne across the table from him than in paying attention to Erna.

Surely it was only an odd distortion of the lighting or his angled perspective that had made the bowl appear to float.

Erna murmured a sighful, "Thank you, Frederick," as she took her place at the head of the table. "Now, then, who would care for leek soup? Olga made it fresh today after our visit to the market."

"Offer them some more Appel Spitz, dear," the other sister suggested. She smiled at Erich over the top of her wineglass. "Erna and I always have a glass or two in the evening. Good for the blood, you know."

Erich also suspected their beverage of choice made the Sisters a little tipsy. Perhaps it had affected him, as well, if he was now seeing tureens of soup floating through the air. "I think I've had enough, thank you."

"It's potent, isn't it?" Julianne met his gaze. A smile teased at the corners of her lips and amusement sparkled in her eyes like refracted light from the crystal chandelier.

"More potent than one might suspect," he agreed. Julianne, too, had a heady effect on him. The dress she wore was a simple one, yet the splashes of bright color made him think of a meadow filled with spring flowers bursting into bloom. A place where you'd want to spread a blanket on the ground, watch the birds soar lazily in a blue sky, and inhale the fragrance of the warm earth. And touch a woman's soft flesh.

He didn't suppose Julianne was beautiful in the classic sense, but her vibrancy shone through in her smile and the naturally high color that tinged her cheeks. If she wore makeup at all, she applied it with artful skill.

Erna ladled a generous serving of soup into a bowl. "There you are, dear boy. Eat hearty. There will be veal and dumplings in a minute. What a shame we have not thought to have you to dinner before."

"I doubt the Langlois have ever socialized with the Berkers," he stated flatly. His ancestors would not have been welcome at this table for the past hundred and fifty years. Nor would he have accepted the invitation had he not needed to prove Frederick's innocence. Even when hungry, the Langlois had learned to fill their plates with pride.

"Pshaw. We shall correct that oversight right now," Erna assured him. "You are always welcome here, Erich. We are neighbors, after all."

"Perhaps you could even see your way clear to help us entertain our Juli during her stay," Olga suggested. She poured a bit more Appel Spitz into her glass. "We do not get around as well as we used to and certainly we would not want her to become bored with the company of two dotty old women."

"Speak for yourself, sister."

"I love simply being here, Olga," Julianne insisted. "You don't have to entertain—"

"It would be my pleasure." The words were out before Erich could drag them back. He should keep his distance from Julianne. That would be the wise thing to do. But she drew him in the same way that alpine peaks challenged him to explore . . . to learn their secrets and test his will. "There is a beer garden in the village. Some evenings they have live music."

"Perfect!" Olga clapped her hands. "You two young people will have such a good time."

"Did you know our Juli won a dance contest in Minnesota?"

"Charming."

"Wait a minute! I'm not going dancing with Erich," Julianne hastily interjected. "In fact, I've already been invited to the beer garden by someone else."

"Really?" Erich frowned. Had some local farmer already snagged Julianne's interest? Not that he had a right to object, of course, but he found the thought of some other man holding her in his arms disturbing.

"Besides, before we get carried away with any plans," Julianne continued, leveling him a very determined look, "I think you need to tell the Sisters what you'd like to do here in the castle. And why."

The Sisters turned their attention toward him in anticipation. Despite being women in their eighties, from their eager smiles it appeared that they had never met an individual they wouldn't trust. He regretted he might be the first to shatter their innocence.

"Yes, well..." He tried the soup and found it quite palatable. Getting the Sisters to swallow him poking around in their mutual past might be a bit more difficult, even for women as naive as these two. "I believe it is time to set aside the nonsense about Frederick Langlois being a witch."

"What a lovely idea! That wild story has gone on far too long as it is. Particularly when he is such a nice man."

Erich noted how Erna used the present tense when referring to Frederick, but let it slide. "There are some Langlois journals in your library. I'd like an opportunity to browse through them."

Olga beamed him a smile. "How nice! That would mean you would be here at the castle often and have a chance to visit with our little Juli."

"That's not the point," Julianne objected. She wasn't about to let him get off so easily and Erich knew it.

"Perhaps she would even be willing to help you with your research," Erna suggested.

"I don't intend to help Erich do anything until you both understand what might happen if he finds what he's looking for."

"Although I'd certainly enjoy her company, Julianne's assistance is entirely unnecessary." And unwanted, he realized. Having a Berker looking over his shoulder every moment would be a definite distraction, particularly if that member of the clan were both attractive and potentially untrustworthy.

"This isn't going to work." Barely suppressing a colorful swear word she'd learned from the hotel's elevator repairman, Julianne tossed her napkin onto the table. She would *not* let Erich take advantage of two, sweet, little old ladies who appeared absolutely determined to put their whole way of life at risk. *And* interfere with her personal life in the process. She didn't *want* to go with Erich to the local beer garden.

She wanted... Oh, damn, she didn't dare want that. Not some guy with penetrating blue eyes looking at her as if he intended her to be dessert. And he looked hungry. *Very* hungry.

Her mouth suddenly dry, she sipped a bit of sweet wine, but it did little to tame her wildly vacillating thoughts.

"Grandma, if Erich is able to clear Frederick's name, he plans to go to the magistrate about it. It might mean you could lose the castle."

The older woman blinked behind thick lenses. "Dear, I think you are overreacting. I am quite sure Frederick would not permit such a thing."

"If Frederick really is..." Erich paused. "How shall we say...stuck on this plane of existence because of the terrible thing that happened to him so long ago, then clearing his name would allow him to go on to..." He shrugged. "Wherever. As I understand it, ghosts only remain until they are released from their earthly ties."

Erna paled. "No. He would not allow that."

"Of course he is *deceased*," Olga said. "How else could he be a ghost?"

"I said *released*," Erich muttered.

"Your battery must be running low, sister. Did you put in a new one?"

"Don't fuss so about my battery. I can hear you just fine." Olga shoved back her chair. "I will bring in the schnitzel."

Rolling her eyes, Julianne wondered how anyone could carry on a decent conversation with the Sisters. Surely they didn't understand what was at stake.

"Then you approve of my plans, Frau Berker?" Erich asked. "To clear Frederick's name?"

"You do as you think you must, dear boy," Erna replied, distractedly smoothing her silver hair.

Without a bit of warning, Erich's soup bowl tipped and the remaining contents spilled into his lap.

He shot to his feet. "What the he—" His chair fell over backward.

"Oh, my, are you all right?" Olga asked from the kitchen door.

"Here, use my napkin, dear. I do hope you are not hurt."

"What happened?" Julianne's questioning gaze met his from across the table.

"I don't know." Dumbfounded, he looked at the wet stain on his dark slacks and the chair that had fallen to the floor behind him. "I must have bumped the edge of the bowl..." But Erich knew he hadn't done any such thing. He'd been sitting there quietly and the damn bowl had flown off the table, dumping its contents into his lap. Thank God the soup hadn't been hot or it sure as hell would have unmanned him. "If I didn't know better, I would think there is someone in this household who doesn't want me examining Frederick's journals too carefully."

"Nonsense, young man."

"We are delighted to have you in our household." Olga's smile was beatific as she vanished into the adjacent room to retrieve the main course for supper.

JULIANNE SELECTED a Langlois journal from a bookshelf in the library and blew a cloud of dust from the top. She hadn't intended to be lured into participating in Erich's search for the truth. All during dinner, however, it had become abundantly clear the Sisters had a different idea. Julianne felt very much as if she had been thrown to the lions—or in this case, to the local dragon.

No way would she allow the Sisters' blatant match-making efforts to put at risk their future here in Schloss Lohr.

Ducking past Erich, she moved to the far side of the desk. "What do you expect to find in these journals?" She felt his eyes following her. So did the telltale scent of leather and spice, uniquely his own.

"I'm not sure." The few lamps in the room cast appealing shadows across his face, emphasizing rugged angles and planes, giving him a mysterious air. In some subliminal way there was the feeling of a predator about him, a man capable of swift, cold blooded actions. "It's possible he made note of activities in the village that were suspicious. Or maybe he realized he was going to be framed by Egon Berker and had enough wisdom to provide us with the truth."

"Are you going to have to read all these journals?" The possibility was daunting.

"Unfortunately, my ancestor organized his notes by topic. Thus far I have found none that are specifically entitled 'The Berker Conspiracy,' so the answers I seek could be anywhere."

"You certainly don't think much of my ancestor, do you?"

"No. The distrust the Langlois have developed for the Berker clan has been many generations in the making."

"Do you include me in that scathing generalization?"

"Only time will make the answer to that question clear."

She eyed him suspiciously. No one got away with challenging her integrity. "So that's why you weren't eager for me to help you out on this little project? You don't trust me?"

He shrugged. "If I were to find evidence—"

"You could alter it." The same way her boss at the hotel had changed signatures on the convention contracts with the plumbers and lingerie distributors, protecting his own job while throwing the blame on her.

A muscle rippled in his jaw. "I could say the same about you."

"All the more reason why we'd better learn to work together. Because I don't trust you, Erich Langlois. You might be willing to go to any lengths to clear your family name. And unless I see for myself—"

Affronted, he said, "You think *I* would lie—"

"That's what you think about me, isn't it?" She planted her fist on her hip. The tension of distrust fairly crackled between them, along with an equally potent current of sexual awareness. He was so damn good-looking, black hair skimming his collar, with a lock that occasionally slipped across his forehead. Strong jaw. Expressive eyes that narrowed and darkened. Dangerously attractive when dressed in unrelenting black and seen against a backdrop of mahogany paneling and ancient leather-bound books. A true lord of the manor. "I have to protect the best interests of my grandmother."

"And I have my sister to worry about."

"Fine. Then we'll keep this search of yours on a level playing field. I go where you go. I see what you see. Any evidence turns up—supporting either family—we both are witnesses."

"That seems a bit extreme."

"It's to your advantage. If we find something that proves your case, I'll be the one—a Berker—who blows the whistle and tells the whole village." Potentially putting her grandmother's future at risk, she worried. "If you pop up with something on your own, who will believe you? You could be making it all up."

"Just as I made up having the bowl of soup fall into my lap? Someone else gets the credit for that mischief."

Her scrutiny shifted to the front of his pants, noting in spite of her best efforts not to, the telling bulge where the fabric pulled tautly across his lean hips. She dragged her gaze back to his stern face, his shadowed jaw and penetrating blue eyes.

"Surely you're not blaming the Sisters for the soup you spilled."

"I only know I did nothing that would cause the bowl to tip into my lap."

"But neither of them was anywhere near you."

"Perhaps, then, you are at fault." He slanted her a speculative glance. "Perhaps 'tis the Berkers who have the power of witchcraft to cast spells over helpless men, not the Langlois. If that's the case, levitating a soup bowl would have been easy." His voice dropped half an octave, sending a chill down her spine. "Or making a man forget the purpose of his visit."

She sputtered, "I—I don't cast spells."

"I'm not so sure... Julianna." The way he said her name, extending each syllable in a richly accented whisper, heated her cheeks and raised her temperature several degrees.

He certainly had an uncanny ability to catch her off guard with his sexual innuendo and volatile moods, first angry and then so sexy it did wild and wonderful things to her insides. She had vowed to be tough when it came to men from now on. With little effort, Erich made that private oath a lie.

Turning, Erich chose the next of Frederick's volumes from the shelf, one that appeared to deal with the production records of milk cows. He realized he had little choice but to accept Julianne's help with the search for clues. His eventual ability to use her as a witness proved to be a compelling argument, though he didn't cherish the prospect of spending long hours in her company. She was far too tempting a morsel and her tongue too quick for his ease of mind. Imagine, a woman who had the effrontery to say she didn't trust him.

He climbed mountains with others depending upon his trustworthiness and the strength of a single rope. How dare this wisp of a woman doubt him?

And what kind of traitor to the Langlois clan had he become that he found her so thoroughly intriguing? Indeed, it was entirely possible she *had* cast a spell over him. She certainly possessed the power.

"I expect you'll find the reading of Frederick's journals to be heavy going," he commented, still thinking he might discourage her unwelcome assistance. And the temptation she represented. "His handwriting is abysmal."

Behind him, near the windows to the library, Erich heard a sound that fell somewhere between a grunt and a burp.

Wide-eyed, Julianne looked at him as though he had been the source of the unpleasant noise. "Are you all right?"

"Fine, thank you." He looked over his shoulder. "It must have been a shutter slamming."

With a skeptical nod, she said, "I imagine I'll be able to read the journals as well as you can. I've been reading hotel reservation slips for years."

"In German?" he questioned.

"And a few in Greek and Italian, too."

She curled up at one end of a leather couch and folded her legs up under her in a thoroughly feminine manner. In contrast to the large piece of furniture, she looked both fragile and vulnerable. Thoroughly appealing. Her every gesture had a subtle grace, even her awkward wielding of a sword, Erich mused. The memory brought an unexpected smile to his lips. She was no doubt the most fascinating woman he had ever met.

Though he avoided initiating contacts with the opposite sex here in Lohr am See, he'd had ample opportunity elsewhere to judge their worth. Julianne, he suspected, would stand out in any crowd, if not for beauty, then for other attributes fully as absorbing.

Given she was a Berker, he tried not to consider just how inviting those virtues could be.

Preparing to settle in for an evening's work at the desk where a lamp provided good light for reading, he swiveled the chair, sat down—

And found himself landing hard on his butt.

"Oh hell!"

Julianne looked up from the journal in her hands to find Erich nowhere in sight.

He shot to his feet. "Is that your idea of a joke?" he bellowed.

"What on earth is the matter now?"

"You pulled the damn chair out from under me."

"I did not!"

"Then how do you explain the fact I just ended up sitting on my back end?" The muscles of his neck corded; his ruddy complexion took on a definite reddish hue and his eyes darkened with fury.

"The chair's on wheels, isn't it? You probably shoved it back without realizing—"

He splayed his hands on the desk, leaning toward her as though prepared to leap down her throat. "I did no such thing."

He looked ferocious enough to breathe fire, but Julianne had no intention of backing down. No wicked dragon was going to intimidate her. "Then maybe the ghost of Frederick Langlois didn't care for your comments about his handwriting."

"That's nonsense."

Remembering the visitor in her room who had admonished her about her housekeeping duties, Julianne was less sure about the resident ghost now than she would have been only a week ago. "Well, I certainly didn't pull your chair out from under you. How could I from across the room?"

His glower lowered into a determined frown. "I don't know. Tricks, I suppose."

"Just like the soup?"

"Yes."

"If that's the case, aren't you risking life and limb by carrying on this investigation? Maybe you ought to call the whole thing off. And leave my poor grandmother alone."

"I am not one to give up so easily, Ms. Berker."

"The name's Olson. My father was third generation American, thank you very much. My *mother,* who I dearly loved, and still miss terribly, was born a Berker and bore her new name as proudly as I do."

Ignoring her comment, he carefully brought the chair back into position and seated himself as gingerly as a man compelled to sit on tacks. He flipped open the journal. "I'm going to clear Frederick's name, with or without your assistance."

"As you wish." She sighed and went back to the heavy diary in her hands. A tiny giggle formed somewhere in her chest and fought for release. What if the culprit in both the case of the soup and the flying chair was really a ghost? However would she explain this adventure to her friends in Minnesota?

In spite of her best efforts, a giggle finally escaped.

Erich looked at her sharply. "Would you care to share the joke with me?"

"No, no." She smothered another laugh that threatened. My, but he was an old sober-sides, and rather adorable even when grumpy. "My mind was just wandering a bit."

Dipping her head, she tried to concentrate on the journal she'd selected from the bookshelf, one that described the plants growing in the local mountains. The swirling handwriting was difficult to read, and some of the words exceeded her language skills, which in no way included a technical vocabulary.

Far worse in terms of distraction was the awareness of Erich sitting behind the desk, the soft sound each time he turned a page, and her wish that they were not destined by generations of ill-will to be enemies.

From even a superficial study of the journal, Julianne discerned Frederick was a botanist, doctor and artist of sorts. He'd painstakingly drawn diagrams of various alpine flowers—their stems, leaves and flowers, even their roots. For each plant he'd noted medicinal properties, if any, and in a few cases whether or not they were poisonous.

Julianne had the feeling this data ought to be looked at by someone far more knowledgeable than she. Based on her viewing of assorted PBS TV shows, the medical community was always looking for folklore about natural curatives.

She was considering that possibility when Erich asked, "Who invited you to the Boar's Head Pub?"

Her head snapped up. The question was so far from where her thoughts had been, she didn't know how to respond. "I beg your pardon?"

"You said you were going to the beer garden. I wondered who had asked you."

A flutter of purely female pleasure shoved a smile onto her face. A curious man meant an interested one. "Just some people I met in the village," she answered casually. No need to mention it was the friendly young woman at the bakery who had sold her strudel that morning and thought Julianne might enjoy what little entertainment there was available in the small community.

"Oh." He ran his palm over his jaw. "I've heard it's a popular place for singles."

"Don't you go there?"

"Rarely."

Strange. She suspected Erich would be very much in demand among the local singles group. "It sounded like fun. I do like to dance." What would it be like, she wondered, to have him as her partner? As a natural athlete, he would be agile. And strong if he were to hold her in his arms. She imagined how she might sway back and forth with him, their bodies touching, the rhythms pulsing—

"You won a contest?"

At the sound of his voice she erased the image of them dancing together as quickly as she would delete an inaccurate accounting statement on a faulty computer. She'd be better off to keep her relationship with Erich on a purely business level. If she could. "Grandma shouldn't have told you that. I was only seven at the time."

His lips curved into a half smile. "I'm sure you were very talented . . . and still are."

"The beer garden is a public place," she observed. "You could drop by this weekend and decide for yourself if I have any talent."

"I'll probably be busy," he replied grumpily.

That managed to deflate her ego. She should know better than to imagine a dark, dangerous hunk would be attracted to her. Clearly something was lacking in her feminine appeal. Though she had dozens of male friends, few had been interested in a serious relationship. Even fewer had interested her in that way. With Erich's obvious distrust of her, he wasn't likely to pursue even friendship.

Not that she wasn't equally suspicious of his motives, she acknowledged.

Erich shot Julianne another curious look, then returned to the task at hand. A cold breeze like the icy fingers of a winter storm slid along the back of his neck. The hair rose on his nape.

Something very strange was going on at Schloss Lohr. He didn't for a moment credit any wild story about a ghost. But a witch's spell? A definite possibility, especially when he considered how thoroughly his thoughts focused on Julianne to the exclusion of his search for the truth.

Even now he found himself intrigued by her small mannerisms. The way the tip of her tongue flicked out to dampen her full lips as she concentrated on the journal. With a lack of self-consciousness, she twirled a bit of silvery blond hair around her finger and he couldn't help wondering how silky that one small curl would feel.

With a muffled groan he returned his attention to the journal on the desk.

He would have to use great care in his dealings with the Berkers. All of them.

And in the future, use extreme caution about where he sat down.

ERNA PRESSED her ear against the door to the library.

"Do you hear anything?" Olga whispered.

"No. It is quite still in there now."

"But we heard shouting a few moments ago. Do you think we should see if they are all right?"

"I think they are better left to their own devices, dear. The young people will work things out."

"I do so love a good romance." Olga sighed. "Do you think we should worry about young Erich looking through Frederick's records? Our Juli seemed concerned."

"No need to trouble yourself, dear. Frederick will take care of matters, I am sure."

"He is quite fond of you, isn't he?"

A tinge of color rose to Erna's cheeks. "Who is that, dear?"

"Do not act so innocent, sister. I mean Frederick, of course."

"I'm quite sure he is equally fond of you." Erna straightened her skirt and fussed with the collar on her blouse. "And it is a comfort to have a man in the house, is it not?"

"It is, indeed." Olga gave her cousin a reassuring smile. "Whose bed he reposes in is of no concern to me."

"Sister!"

They gazed at each other, then broke into gales of youthful giggles they muffled with their hands.

Chapter Five

The car careered to a halt outside a small roadside restaurant and Julianne let out a relieved sigh. As a tour guide, Erna certainly provided some exciting moments. Particularly when she was behind the wheel of her old Mercedes sedan.

"We will stop for a bit of a refreshment here," Erna said over her shoulder, "before we drive on home." The car lurched as she momentarily mistook "reverse" for "park" on the gear lever.

"Iced tea and a piece of strudel, perhaps?" Olga questioned. "Herr Scheiblberger, the bakery chef here, makes a lovely pastry. Almost as flaky as mine."

"You should have been a professional chef, Olga. You're a wonderful cook."

"I have often thought so myself," Erna agreed. She glanced over her shoulder at Julianne in the back seat. "In fact, after we were both widowed, we considered turning Schloss Lohr into a small hotel."

That possibility caught Julianne's interest.

"But we didn't know how to begin," Olga said.

"And dear Frederick truly did not approve. So we gave up the idea."

As Julianne got out of the car, she imagined her grandmother's castle as an inn and smiled. But the car pitched forward again when Erna turned off the ignition, and Julianne had to jump clear. She decided it would be wise if she volunteered to drive the next leg of their journey. That is, if she wanted to survive her vacation in one piece.

Since Erich had announced he had other plans for the day, she'd had no interest in pursuing the laborious task of reading Frederick's journals on her own. A break after three days of reading dry, plotless technical notes would do them both good.

So the Sisters had taken the opportunity to drive her across the border into Germany for a visit to Berchtesgaden and the surrounding national park. It had been a lovely day, sunny and warm, but strangely Julianne had missed spending the time with Erich.

As they got out of the car, high-pitched, childish laughter came from an adjacent playground, drawing Julianne's attention. A gaggle of youngsters stood at the base of a manmade mountain watching a young boy struggling to climb a vertical wall. A skinny kid, he didn't seem to have the strength to pull himself up to the next artificial outcropping of rock. Only a harness and safety rope prevented him from falling.

Even watching from a distance caused sweat to break out on Julianne's palms. Climbing mountains was definitely not a recreational activity she'd voluntarily choose.

"You can do it, Konrad," encouraged the man who supervised the children. "Think first, then reach for the next hold. Move slowly. There's no rush."

Julianne smiled at the sound of his familiar voice. So this was what Erich had been up to that had taken him away from Lohr am See for the day.

"Easy now," he called. "You're doing fine. Keep your back straight."

"Herr Langlois, can I try next?" asked a girl in the crowd.

"You'll get your turn. I promise."

Without actually intending to, Julianne strolled toward Erich and his students. She hadn't thought of him as a teacher, but clearly the kids did. They fidgeted like all children do, while at the same time they seemed well disciplined. To her surprise, she realized Erich looked more at ease with these children than she had ever seen him at Lohr am See, certainly more comfortable than he was among his own villagers.

"I did it!" the youngster called when he reached the top of the wall. "I really did it!"

"We knew you could, Konrad. Didn't we, *Jugends*?" he asked the class.

Right on cue, the children sent up an appreciative cheer for Konrad.

Julianne's eyes met Erich's surprised gaze across the top of the youngsters. Caught gawking, she flushed.

"Hi," she mouthed.

He spoke softly to one of the taller boys, handed him the safety rope that was still attached to young Konrad, then came in her direction.

An amused twinkle sparkled in his eyes, as though he was glad to see her, and her heart did one of the amazing somersaults that seemed to happen whenever Erich was around.

"I wasn't aware you'd signed up for my class in rock climbing."

"Oh, no, not me." She gestured vaguely over her shoulder. "The Sisters have just given me a tour of Berchtesgaden. We stopped for a snack."

He nodded. "You're welcome to join the class, if you'd like."

"I'd have to start off in the remedial class. I don't even like climbing a stepladder."

His laughter came easily, as warm as the summer sunshine, and this relaxed Erich seemed like a totally different man than the grim dragon she'd seen so often before. His smile was a devastatingly masculine flash of white and his cheeks creased with humor.

"I gather you like working with children," she said, fascinated by this new and unexpected vision of Erich.

"It gives me a chance to encourage others to explore the mountains and appreciate them for both their beauty and their serenity. Young people need to be physically challenged. The Alps provide that and more."

"Do you take kids on actual climbing expeditions?"

"When I can. It's a good, wholesome experience for young people. Better than spending their days watching television. Or even playing rugby, for that matter."

"You sound like a missionary."

"I'm always looking for converts." He eyed her up and down, lazily taking in the way her jeans flared over her hips and gloved her slender legs. "Are you sure you don't want a lesson? I could arrange a private session."

She swallowed hard. In private, she imagined Erich could teach her a good many subjects, few of them related to climbing, but all of them exciting. "I'll pass. Thanks. Do you teach a class in Lohr am See, too?"

His smile dissolved. "Not likely."

"But why—" Of course, she realized with a start, the villagers wouldn't approve of a Langlois doing anything in their community. At least, not a Langlois who glowered at them, and perhaps they didn't know about this other man who could be so patient with children.

From the restaurant Erna called, "Juli, dear, they have a table ready for us."

"I have to go," she told Erich.

"I will see you tomorrow morning, then? At the castle?"

A shiver of anticipation crept down her spine. "Yes." Her response was a husky whisper. Having seen Erich in a gentler, kinder light would make him all that more difficult to resist. *If* he ever indicated any interest, that is. With a mental sigh of regret, she forced herself to remember he was still the man determined to take over her grandmother's castle. "I'll see you in the morning."

THE TANTALIZING scent of yeasty bread dough surrounded Erich as he entered the castle kitchen, filling him with nostalgic memories he hadn't thought about in years.

As he had for the past week, with the exception of the day before, he'd come to Schloss Lohr at midmorning to resume the search through Frederick's journals. But today, instead of escorting him to the library, the Sisters had directed him to the kitchen where Julianne was literally up to her elbows in flour. The counters were similarly covered with an avalanche of fine white powder, and it appeared every bowl and stirring spoon owned by the Sisters had been put to use.

Chaos. An anarchy such as he had never before witnessed. To a life of order, Julianne Olson brought the *föhn* wind feared in ancient Austrian legends because it could easily drive a man mad. In her case, a man might go willingly.

His lips twitched into a wry smile. "I gather cooking is not one of your many and varied talents."

She jumped at his voice. "Oh, no, I love to cook." She returned his smile, looking fully as delicious as the raisin-filled dough she held in her hands. The T-shirt she wore emphasized small, delicate breasts, and was tucked in at a narrow waist to jeans that clung to her rounded hips. "Olga's got a wonderful Bavarian recipe for braided bread, and I had to try it."

"I shall assume, then, that Frederick the ghost, or some other equally mischievous poltergeist, has gone on a rampage with the sole purpose of creating havoc. How else could you explain all this?" His gesture included the entire kitchen.

"Only a real artist can make this big a mess. But it'll be delicious. You'll see." Laughing, she placed the ball of dough in the bowl, turned, then kneaded it with the heels of her hands. "I meant to have all this done and in the oven before you came. But I got to visiting with the Sisters."

"They do love to talk, don't they?" He watched in admiration as she worked the dough, his groin tightening as he wondered what her hands would feel like kneading his flesh. Or caressing him even more gently. He'd been surprised to see her yesterday at the playground. And secretly pleased.

"Hmm." She dropped the ball onto a floured board and began dividing it into sections. "This part of the job won't take long. Then we can get back to work in the library."

"There's no hurry." In fact, Erich rather liked watching Julianne in the kitchen. He'd had no idea she was so domestic, though he had given the possibility little thought until now. Admittedly he tended to categorize women. He'd already begun to suspect Julianne wouldn't fit into any of his neat definitions. He doubted any single label would fit her completely and was startled to find how much that surprised him.

"Here." She shoved one of the smaller balls of dough into his hands. "Roll it into a snake about a foot or so long."

"I don't know how to make bread," he protested.

With a puff, she tried to blow a few flyaway strands of silver blond hair from her forehead. When that failed, she wiped at them with the back of her hand, leaving a streak of flour that matched the smudge that was already on the tip of her nose. An intriguing spot Erich had the oddest desire to kiss.

He'd been troubled by similar urges all too often of late, he reminded himself sternly. Urges he fought to resist.

"There's nothing hard about rolling out dough," she insisted with eager encouragement in her eyes. "Come on. It'll go faster with the two of us working."

As she proceeded to roll out the first bit of dough, Julianne noted Erich quickly caught the rhythm once he learned to flour his hands as well as the board. Given enough experience, he'd probably make a darn good baker. Working carefully, he didn't overknead the dough, and that was important. In an unexpected flight of fancy, she imagined he'd treat a woman with the same care.

"My mother used to bake bread." There was a note of nostalgia in his voice as he picked up a second ball and began shaping it on the board. His fingers were long and tapered, strong and gentle at the same time. "I remember how I loved to come home from school and find the kitchen smelling of freshly baked bread."

She risked treading on sensitive ground. "The Sisters told me your mother wasn't well from the time you were quite young."

"They're right. She couldn't handle the social ostracism of the villagers. When they married, my father had hoped she would be stronger. But then, I doubt one in a thousand women would have survived what she went through."

"What happened to her?" Julianne asked softly.

"The children in the village made up songs about the Langlois and trailed along behind her on market day taunting her. Occasionally the bolder ones would throw stones at her."

Julianne's heart ached in response to the woman's pain. "That's terrible! Couldn't your father stop them?"

"He couldn't be with her every waking moment. He had his own work to do. Eventually she withdrew entirely and never went outside the house. Or opened the shutters, for that matter." His hands stilled on the doughy log he'd made. "When Helene was two, Mama left us."

"You mean, she died?"

"No. She simply left. One morning we woke up and she was gone."

Sympathy welling up and crowding around her heart, Julianne covered his hand. She'd always been a sucker for a sad story. She cried in practically every movie she saw, and was forever bringing home stray puppies, or hotel employees down on their luck. Her mother had done the same sort of thing with transients who'd been looking for work around their farm. "I'm sorry," she said simply.

"For a long time I expected her to come back. I couldn't believe she would desert me and my sister. My father, of course, knew better."

"He could have gone after her. Or you all could have moved somewhere else."

He lifted his chin proudly. Almost arrogantly. But she could still see the boyhood hurt in his eyes. "The Langlois belong here. At Lohr am See. Mother should have understood that. But rest assured, I have no intention of putting any woman through the same pain she experienced."

"You mean, you're never going to marry?"

"Never. It would be too cruel a punishment for any woman."

"But if you clear the Langlois name, surely you'd consider marrying then."

His gaze swept over her face in a slow perusal that caused a race of heat to her cheeks. She never should have asked such a personal question. His plans for the future were none of her business.

"Do you think there are those who might be interested?" he asked softly.

"A few." Her voice cracked. A few thousand was closer to the truth. Not that she'd count herself among that number. But, Lord, he was the devil's own temptation.

"It would be a disservice for me to marry any woman. Even under the best of circumstances, the prejudices of the villagers are likely to last a long time. It would be too much for a woman to endure."

"Maybe you underestimate how strong a woman can be." Or how strangely weak a woman's knees could feel when she looked into the depth of his troubled blue eyes.

A charged silence filled the kitchen, heating the room as though a second oven had been switched on. His hands paused on the dough, his penetrating gaze searching for...something.

"Did you know you have a smudge of flour on the end of your nose?" He reached up with a single finger, coming so close she imagined she could feel his heat and the roughened swirls of his fingerprint.

She swallowed hard. "No."

"I'd wipe it off but I'm afraid I'd make more of a mess than is already there." Dropping his hand, he slowly dipped his head toward hers. "Fortunately, I can think of an alternate way to remove the smudge."

"You can?" So could she, and she trembled in anticipation, rising slightly on her toes to provide better access for his alluring lips.

The kitchen door swung open. "There you two are," Olga said, bursting into the room. "How is the bread coming along?"

They jumped apart as though a flame had leapt out of the hot oven to scorch them.

Julianne had to draw a steadying breath before she spoke. "Almost ready for the final rising," she announced. From the way Erich had turned his back on Olga, she suspected other things had been rising, too. In her case they'd certainly been heating up.

"Ach, how nice. Then we must sheath the loaf in a deliciously smooth glaze. I can hardly wait to taste it." Olga beamed them a smile.

Julianne nearly choked, her mind still traveling down forbidden paths. This was no time to be thinking about sheaths or intimate flavors. She really needed to get a handle on her wayward thoughts, including images of hot, sweaty bodies. His. Hers. Together. Shielded by only a down comforter.

Never in Minnesota had her mind been so filled with erotic notions. But then, maybe she'd been too busy working to permit so many illicit ideas to enter her head.

At the sink, Erich washed the sticky dough from his hands. Cold water sluiced over his fingers in the same chilling way Olga's untimely arrival had shocked him back to some semblance of reality.

He hadn't intended to reveal intimate details of his past to Julianne. Nor had he planned to kiss her. Only outside intervention had halted that impulsive act.

Never had he met a woman so easy to talk to. Without apparent effort she encouraged confidences he'd never shared with anyone else. That was dangerous. He was a man used to being alone. With the exception of his devotion to his sister, he preferred it that way.

Like a skilled climber finding handholds where none appeared to be, Julianne revealed tiny crevices within his psyche he hadn't known existed. He suspected there was a deep core of strength hidden behind Julianne's apparent innocence, and wondered if she was the one woman who could look past the rumors and innuendos that had plagued the Langlois for years and see the man inside. He wanted to open up to her, to accept the gentle probe of her fingertips, but he didn't dare. As much for her sake as his own.

"I'd best get started in the library," he said, drying his hands on a nearby towel. "You can come along whenever you're finished here."

Julianne bent over the ropes of dough, twining one with another. Erich had the distinct impression she was avoiding meeting his gaze.

"I'll be right there," she said.

"It is a shame you two must lock yourselves away in our dusty old library on such a beautiful day." Olga slipped a floral bib apron over her dress. "Why do you not do something outside to enjoy the sun while you can?"

"We took yesterday off," he stated.

"Ah, but the sun will not last. It never does. You should take advantage of the good weather while you can."

"We're not making much progress reading those journals," Julianne admitted. "I'm learning more about the local flora and fauna than I really wanted to know."

"I'm learning a few juicy tidbits about the neighbors, too. But nothing that appears of particular value."

"Well, then, that settles matters," Olga insisted. "I will fix you a picnic lunch and Erich will show you our countryside. He is a guide, you know." The older woman smiled brightly at Erich. "She thought you worked in a *bar,* though how she got such a notion I have no idea."

"I didn't, Olga. You were the one—"

"Why would I say such a foolish thing? I have always known Erich was a guide. A very fine one, too, I understand."

"Yes, b-but—" Julianne sputtered in exasperation. "The other day in the car—"

"Now, now, dear, we all make mistakes. Do not let it trouble you. I will finish up here and prepare your lunch while you clean up a bit."

Julianne caught Erich's eye with a questioning look. She'd just as soon be outside on such a terrific day rather than stuck inside. Besides, being confined to the library alone with Erich was beginning to feel far too intimate. And their near kiss only moments ago had stirred up feelings she didn't want to examine too closely. Surely a little exercise would cool off her imagination.

"I had considered visiting the site where they claim the witches' coven met," he said. "Even after all this time it might provide us with some insight into what happened so long ago."

A shiver ran down her spine. "There's really a place like that?"

"It's part of the local folklore. They claim on nights with a full moon you can see the ghosts of burned witches dancing in a circle and hear them chanting their evil spells."

Watching Olga deftly twist the second layer of dough ropes together, Julianne said, "Sounds like a wonderful place to visit on a bright sunny day." But definitely not at night. The very idea gave her the willies.

"Not many of the villagers care to go there at all," he said. "They're a superstitious lot."

"Fortunately I'm not." Or at least Julianne hadn't been until she'd arrived at Schloss Lohr.

Olga draped a towel over the finished bread to keep it warm while the yeast did its work. "Now then, there was sausage left over from supper last night. And some strudel. There's cheese, too. I will make up something nice for you."

"I'll pick up some wine in the village," Erich offered.

"You don't have to go to so much trouble, Olga," Julianne said.

"Shoo, shoo." Olga waved her away from the worktable. "I will put in a nice bottle of Appel Spitz for your picnic, *ja?*"

"Erich just said he'd get some wine," Julianne said loudly.

The older woman looked surprised. "Oh, well, go wash yourself up and by then the picnic will be ready. If he wants to take *twine* on a picnic, it is fine with me."

Julianne rolled her eyes. She'd leave Erich to deal with Olga's most recent misunderstanding.

Escaping the kitchen, she imagined that if she didn't clean the smudge of flour from her nose, she'd be asking for trouble. Erich had seemed far too tempted to take care of the problem with his own unique methods.

And she was unfairly eager to let him.

After she had changed clothes and put on some hiking shoes, she found Erich in the library. A column of sunlight poured through rippling windowpanes to cast a checkerboard pattern on the hardwood floor. Erich stood looking outside, one of Frederick's journals in his hand, a troubled expression on his face.

"What's wrong?" she asked.

"I've found a book of recipes."

"What's so awful about that? Maybe there's a secret recipe for Bavarian chocolate," she suggested brightly. "We could copyright it and make a fortune."

A scowl wrinkled his forehead and lowered his brows. Whatever he'd found wasn't a joke.

"I don't think there is much of a market for a concoction of ground toad skin and pine bark."

Her stomach instantly agreed. "That's in Frederick's journal? Ground-up toads?"

"Along with similar and equally repulsive recipes. About the only one I can't find is a compound using eye of newt."

"Why would your ancestor—"

"It sounds like typical witches' brew to me." He paced across the room and tossed the journal onto the desk. It landed with a condemning thud. "It is possible Frederick was indeed tinkering with witchcraft."

"But he wasn't a *witch*. He couldn't have been. Witches didn't exist then, and they don't now."

"You may be right, but unless I can explain away the entries in this journal, a court would undoubtedly rule the archbishop had been within his rights to punish Frederick Langlois for dabbling in the occult. The confiscation of his lands would stand."

It seemed terribly unfair that the future of Schloss Lohr should rest on a useless recipe created more than a hundred years ago. Except some tidbit of information was rattling around in the back of Julianne's mind trying to get loose. She was hardly an expert on toads, so she had no idea what was troubling her and shrugged off the feeling.

"Come on," Erich said. "Olga has probably prepared our picnic by now. Maybe we'll find the answers up in the mountains where the witches' coven used to meet."

Chapter Six

Peaceful.

Julianne felt the silence stretch on filaments of air from the secluded alpine meadow to the top of the snow-covered peaks that surrounded it. As far as she could tell, no other human existed in the entire universe. Only she and Erich, chaperoned by soaring ravens caught up in the lifting currents sweeping along the steep cliffs, were a part of the dramatically framed grotto.

The hike here had been long but not particularly arduous. Though overgrown, the trail had been wide enough that Julianne's fear of heights had been kept at bay and she was grateful she hadn't made a fool of herself with a man who climbed mountains for a living.

Still, they had climbed high enough into the hills that the air seemed thin and far cooler than it had been in the valley.

"Amazing," Julianne whispered, afraid to disturb the solitude. The ground was carpeted with splashes of purple and yellow and green, the air filled with the sweet scent of wildflowers and new grass. "After reading Frederick's journals, I feel like I've been here before."

From memory, she identified purple harebells and monkshood, and the bright yellow of arnica. In sheltered spots, pink moss campion provided soft punctuation to the brighter flowers that filled the meadow. If ancient witches had come here to share their secrets, they had indeed selected a mystical place.

"There are a thousand miniature meadows in the Alps," Erich said. "Each one is unique."

"But Frederick was here. I'm sure of it."

"It's possible."

Her gaze swept the ground, then climbed the cliffs. "I don't see any edelweiss."

"The flower for which Austria is so well known grows at a much higher altitude than this meadow. That's why bringing a woman a sprig of edelweiss has become a foolish romantic tradition in our country. It's not easily obtained."

"Olga was certainly proud that her late husband had made the effort when they were courting."

"As I say, a foolish custom."

She shot him a curious look. "In addition to being a confirmed bachelor, I gather you're not the romantic sort?"

"I see little difference between edelweiss and a bunch of daisies."

"Well, I do. If a guy risked his neck climbing a mountain to bring me back anything at all, I'd be impressed. A woman appreciates the kind of man who's willing to go that extra mile.''

He acknowledged her comment with a condescending nod that suggested he'd be the last man on earth to indulge that kind of a romantic whim. Not that he'd need to, Julianne mused. No doubt he'd have plenty of women at his beck and call without making much of an effort.

Julianne walked into the center of a circle of raised granite blocks, each of them three or four feet high, some sporting a mantel of moss.

At her nape she felt the tug of an electric shiver. ''This is the place, isn't it? Where witches once danced?''

''So they say. These small monoliths are said to be not unlike those at Stonehenge or in the Easter Islands.''

Cupping her elbows, she hugged her arms to her midsection. Rocks didn't have any intrinsic power. Yet she felt something pulling her, a mystical gravity that was hard to ignore.

Or maybe she was feeling the timbre of Erich's deeply accented voice spooling down her spine, the heady intoxication of his leathery scent mixing with that of the wildflowers. The combination had her off-balance, wanting things she couldn't even define. He might not believe in romance, but he certainly had an amorous effect on her.

''What's that building?'' she asked, shifting her attention to the low stone structure about eight feet square that stood outside the circle. The two visible windows were little more than slits in the dark rock, and the door that stood ajar looked ponderously heavy.

"It's a shelter for mountain climbers should they be caught in a storm."

"Have you ever had to stay there?"

"No. When you get much beyond this point, the climbs are technically very advanced. I rarely have clients who would want such a difficult challenge. And there are other routes to these particular peaks that are more interesting."

"I bet you know every one of these mountains like the back of your hand."

He chuckled. "The Alps are like a woman. The moment you become cocky and think you know all there is to know about her, she surprises you. In the case of these mountains, the unpredictability can be fatal."

"But you love your work." It wasn't a question. She could hear the pride in Erich's voice . . . and his love for the mountains that had become his mistress. Strangely, she felt a sharp stab of envy that he could care so much about inanimate rocks and she wondered why that would bother her.

"I cannot imagine any other way I would want to make my living."

"You're a lucky man to be doing what you want to with your life." Though initially, she realized, the censure of the villagers might well have been the impetus that drove him to the mountains to seek his own counsel.

She turned to walk out of the mystical circle, but before she could escape he caught her hand.

"Have you heard the story of the *föhn* wind we have here in Austria?"

"I don't think so."

"Sometimes during the winter months a warm wind blows up from the south. It's such an unusual phenomena, and can affect people so strangely, that men have used the wind as a defense in murder trials, much like a plea of temporary insanity." He pulled her toward him, gently curling his arm behind her back, bringing their bodies together in a tender impact of male against female, soft against hard. "In spite of all my efforts to prevent it, you affect me in the same way, Julianna."

She swallowed hard. "You mean, you're planning murder?"

"No. What I have in mind is far more foolish than that."

His words, spoken so softly, with such underlying passion, cast an immobilizing spell over Julianne. Her body felt heavy, in contrast to a new light-headedness, and her legs seemed incapable of movement. So she waited as the mystical moment of anticipation shimmered through the clear alpine air.

There must be enchantment in the witches' circle, she thought dimly, closing her eyes as he dipped his head toward hers.

His lips were warmer than she had expected, molding to hers in a perfect fit. First at one angle and then another, he explored their matching shapes and the spellbound heat of shared wanting.

His tongue slid along the seam of her lips. As though the moist instrument was a magic wand, she opened to his penetration. His kiss engaged every part of her mouth in a sensual adventure, long and hot and wet. He sipped and stroked and nipped, teasing and testing her response.

While still holding her captive against the long length of his body, his other hand caressed the sensitive column of her neck. His fingers wove through her hair. He possessed her in thought, if not yet in deed.

Time fled, marked only by Julianne's racing heartbeat and the rapid rhythm of her breathing.

Finally, in some small, still-rational part of her mind, Julianne recognized Erich as a wizard of seduction. Practiced and patient, everything he did was designed to arouse, to tantalize and tempt.

And he was the man set on taking Schloss Lohr away from her grandmother. A man who very likely was no more trustworthy than her boss at the hotel had been, at least when it came to matters of the heart.

With her free hand she palmed Erich's chest and felt his heart beating as thunderously as her own. It was all she could do not to curl her fingers into the soft fabric of his T-shirt, like a cat seeking comfort. Groaning in frustration, she shoved ineffectually at his greater size.

''We can't do this,'' she pleaded, dragging her lips away from his.

"I told you my actions would be most unwise." His eyes had darkened nearly to black. His nostrils flared. "All due to the *föhn* wind that you bring to Lohr am See."

She looked at him quizzically. "Funny, when I first met you I thought of a different folktale."

"Which one is that?"

"Something about a wicked dragon who comes down from the mountains to steal a virgin every fifty years or so."

One corner of his lips hitched into a half smile. "You thought of me as that frightening fellow?"

"Close enough." Definitely dangerous to a woman's peace of mind.

"I take it, then, that you are a virgin?"

A rush of heated blood sped to her cheeks. "That's not something I'm prepared to discuss."

"Ah. A woman's secret." His smile grew broader. "But you think of me as the dragon?"

"When you're angry, you do look like you're about to breathe fire." But not at this particular moment. Right now he simply looked sexy and temptingly handsome, with a smile as gentle as the ones he'd bestowed on the children at the playground. A smile that tugged on Julianne's heart and sent intriguing messages racing through hidden places in her body.

"Then you will be relieved to know that particular dragon resides in the mountains near Salzburg, not here." A teasing light gleamed in his dark eyes. "Though I suppose it's possible he has moved since the tale was first told. Details of that sort are often over-looked."

"Oh, that's very reassuring." Controlling her breathlessness seemed an impossible chore, and her lungs heaved with the effort to drag in high-altitude air. "I also liked your knees at first sight."

His smiled widened, his cheeks creasing in that devastating way. "My knees?"

"Lederhosen can be very titillating on the right man."

"I hadn't realized that."

Neither had she. Until recently.

She slipped away from his grasp, but the heat of him stayed with her. The memory of his kiss. How his fingers had linked with hers. The press of his body and the feel of his arousal against her midsection. Memories she wouldn't soon forget.

Once outside the circle of stones, she felt a little more at ease, as though the magic of the meadow was the most potent where witches had once danced.

Lord, now he had her *believing* in spells and incantations. All because of a single enchanted kiss.

Unrelieved sexual tension thrummed through her, making her restless and pushing her toward the stone shelter, away from Erich and the feelings she wanted to deny. She peered through the open doorway into the gloom. The cramped space smelled damp and cold. Unwelcoming.

Goose bumps tracked down her spine as if a ghost had walked over her grave.

Or materialized out of the shadows.

She wasn't exactly afraid of the dark, but she definitely wouldn't want to spend the night in a place like this, cold weather or not. A neighborhood haunted by witches wasn't a place she'd want to linger.

"It'd take a pretty big storm to get me to stay in this place," she declared. "I prefer my accommodations to be at least four-star. When I can afford it, of course."

"So do I, but there are times when getting out of the wind is the only way to survive. These huts are scattered all across the mountains. Over the years they've saved a good many lives."

"Yours included?" She glanced back to where he still stood in the center of the circle. Caught half in shadow and half in sunlight, he looked mysterious and unknowable. No man in the States, she admitted, had ever seemed so intriguing.

"A storm in the Alps can catch even an experienced guide off guard," he said.

She shivered at the thought Erich might have lost his life in a blizzard before she'd even had a chance to meet him.

As she took a last glance into the hut one of scattered rocks on the floor moved. It actually *moved!* Then it hopped to the far wall and hid in the deepest shadows.

"Erich, there's a toad in here." Her voice cracked on the announcement.

"There are a couple of different varieties in the Alps. They're harmless."

Wonderful. At least this one had avoided being ground up into some sort of a witches' brew by Great-Great-Grandpa Frederick.

"Come. Let's have our lunch." Shrugging off his small day pack, Erich spread a picnic cloth on the ground, then set out the food.

Julianne was happy to join him well away from the dark, dank hut and its current occupant.

"I think Olga planned for us to invite friends to lunch," he said. "There seems to be enough here for Hannibal's army, including his elephants."

"Imagine, trying to conquer Austria by crossing the Alps. The man must have been crazy." She sat down next to the cloth and folded her legs beside her, mashing the springy new grass that served as a cushion.

With the skill of an experienced host at a five-star inn, he pulled the cork on a bottle of red wine. Two plastic glasses that looked very much like crystal magically appeared from his pack. After tasting the wine, he poured a glass for her. "A 1990 vintage. I think you'll like it."

"Very impressive. Up here in the mountains I expected to have to drink my wine out of a bota, which I don't do very well." She accepted the wine and sipped carefully. The bouquet was exquisite, the flavor fruity. "With a bota, I either half drown myself and end up choking to death, or I get the wine sprayed all over my front."

He smiled indulgently. "It's an art form created for the sole purpose of impressing fellow skiers. Do you ski?"

"A little. Everyone in Minnesota does, I suppose."

"In Austria, they say children are born with skis on their feet."

"Ouch! That's gotta be uncomfortable for their mothers."

He laughed, a deep, rich sound that made Julianne think of long winter nights in front of a fire, hot chocolate and warm, fuzzy slippers.

"The only time I visited America, I went to Aspen in Colorado. Do you know the place?"

"Sure. I went there one Christmas vacation while I was in college. It cost an arm and leg to get there, plus the price of the condo ten of us had rented. First day on the slopes I twisted my knee. The view from the condo was wonderful. And not nearly as terrifying as the view from the chair lift."

He did it again—that half smile that sent Julianne's libido into high gear. Combined with a rumble of deep-throated laughter, like a distant avalanche, it would be easy to get caught up in the magic of this meadow. Julianne tried hard to not let that happen.

"So what were you doing in Aspen?" she asked.

"I was on a junior ski team representing Austria."

"Really? How'd you do?"

"I took first in both downhill and giant slalom." As casually as if winning a major race meant nothing, he cut slices of cheese and sausage on a paper plate, then tore off a hunk of French bread, which he handed to Julianne.

"Did you think about trying for the Olympics?"

"Briefly. The truth is, when you're racing downhill you don't have much time to enjoy the scenery. When I climb these mountains..." He looked up at the soaring peaks that he so obviously loved. "The whole world is beneath you. For me, that's a far greater challenge."

"Actually, I'm surprised the whole Lohr valley isn't crisscrossed by ski lifts. This should be wonderful skiing country."

"It would be, and there has been talk of developing the area. But no one's come forward with the financial backing. I'm hopeful that won't ever happen."

She caught a frown in his voice. "You don't approve?"

"They scar the landscape by cutting ski trails through the forest and the lifts are unnatural, all done in the name of bringing cash to the local economy." He took a bite of cheese, then washed it down with wine. "What they don't consider is the down side. Development can actually destroy the livelihoods of the tenant farmers who work the lands owned by people like your grandmother."

"I didn't know that." His thoughtful commentary on the pros and cons of development impressed her. A man who climbed dangerous alpine peaks was not one to jump to hasty conclusions, she imagined. She, on the other hand, tended to operate from instinct. Which had gotten her into trouble more than once.

He sat with his arm resting comfortably on an up-raised knee. Taut denim gloved his muscular thigh.

"Do you expect to have difficulty finding new employment when you return to Minnesota?"

"Not really. But I thought I'd take my time looking." She smiled ruefully. "As long as my savings permit, that is. Instead of a city hotel that caters mostly to businessmen, I'd like to try working at a resort. I'd even consider an upscale country inn."

"You don't like the city?"

"I was raised on an apple farm. I kind of miss the quiet of the countryside." She popped a piece of cheese into her mouth and chewed thoughtfully. "I guess eventually I'd like to manage a small hotel on my own. The big chains have a rather strong preference for men at the top. And frankly, I'm tired of taking orders." Particularly from men willing to take advantage of her.

"I prefer being my own boss, too." His smile brought squint lines to the corners of his eyes. "In my business, no one argues with the man holding the other end of the rope."

She laughed, amazed at how comfortable she felt with Erich, while at the same time aware of her obstinate and foolish desire that their relationship go beyond a single kiss.

"Do your parents approve of your career plans?" he asked amiably.

"My dad does, I guess. Mother died several years ago and last year Dad remarried. She's a wonderful woman, and I wouldn't want Dad to be alone, but somehow he and I don't talk as much as we used to."

"Were you close to your mother?"

"Very. All during my teen years, when other girls were fighting with their moms, my mother was my best friend. I still miss her like crazy. That's probably one of the reasons I thought of visiting Grandma Erna when I quit my job in a huff."

"You wanted a shoulder to cry on?"

She shrugged and smiled a little sadly. "I'd say that was a pretty perceptive observation."

Companionably, they nibbled on chunks of hard sausage and cheese, savoring the taste with wine. She learned the black birds that soared along the side of the cliffs were actually alpine chough, not ravens as she had thought, and her hearing became acute enough to pick up the sound of insects busily at work in the meadow.

She leaned back against one of the stone markers, content and relaxed, and the next thing she felt was the soft caress of Erich's fingertips on her cheek.

She started, her eyes flying open.

"You are quite lovely when you sleep," he said, his voice husky, a smile playing at the edges of his lips as he crouched beside her. "Like Sleeping Beauty."

Julianne knew that wasn't true. She'd never been considered beautiful. Spunky and effervescent, yes. Certainly, being friendly was her hallmark. But beautiful? Not a chance.

"If all Austrian men are born with glib silver tongues like yours to go along with their skis, it's a wonder the women survive."

With another smile, he extended his hand. "Come, my sleeping princess. There's something I want to show you."

"Show me?" She accepted his hand, stood and brushed a few bits of grass off the back of her jeans. Warily she realized there were a good many places she'd be willing to follow Erich.

"There's a spectacular view of the next valley a short distance up the trail. You'll enjoy it."

He led the way out of the witches' circle and Julianne was struck by the rather nice view of his tight buns and muscular thighs. She really shouldn't be thinking about that, she chided herself, but admitted Erich would attract the attention of any female with even less than perfect eyesight.

The path grew steeper and more rocky, though Erich's rapid pace remained constant. Gathering her breath, Julianne let her gaze slide away from him to the terrain.

"Oh, God..." A terrifying paralysis gripped her. Her knees began to quake and her breath came in little pants.

Erich had led her onto a path that edged the mountainside hundreds of feet above a rock-strewn chasm. She'd been so busy admiring her guide, she hadn't noticed where they were going.

Instantly, sweat soaked her palms. Fear accelerated her heart rate. Knees trembling, she plastered her back against the mountainside and squeezed her eyes closed.

"Erich..." Her cry for help was little more than a desperate whisper.

The odd, choked sound halted Erich in his tracks. He turned, puzzled.

All the blood had drained from Julianne's face and she stood rooted in place.

"What's the matter?" he asked, concerned she might be having a heart attack. He hurried to her side.

Slowly she opened her eyes. "I'm..." She licked her lips. "I'm... afraid of heights."

The concept was so foreign to Erich, it took a minute for him to understand what she was saying. From his perspective they were on a simple walking trail that was in no way perilous.

"The path widens a bit around the next corner," he told her. "You'll be fine—"

Wide-eyed, she shook her head. "No, really. I've, uh, got to go back. I'm sorry." Her shoulders flattened against the mountainside, she began to edge back the way they had come.

"You're really that afraid?"

"Silly, isn't it?" She made a brave attempt at a smile. "I can't even look straight down from a second-story window without feeling queasy."

She really was terrified, he realized. That he himself had never experienced fear of heights didn't make the sensation any less frightening to her. In a way, he admired her courage for even trying to follow him up this path.

He took her arm and steadied her. "It's time we were going back anyway. Trust me. I won't let you fall. It would be bad for my reputation as a mountain guide."

Her shaky smile was enough to earn her another badge for bravery in Erich's mind. Admitting one's own fears was never easy.

"Guess I won't ever have a chance to see edelweiss blooming," she said with a nervous laugh as she sidestepped down the trail. Her color was a little better, but he could still feel her trembling. "I'd never in a million years be able to climb up high enough to find any."

"You might want to leave that pleasure to others."

"I will. You can count on it."

BY THE TIME they reached the witches' circle again, and Julianne managed to draw a steady breath, the sun no longer touched the magic meadow and the air had grown noticeably cooler. In the lengthening shadows the circle took on an eerie quality, as though the witches' ghosts were waiting in cracks and crevices for night to arrive so they could put on a show.

This was definitely not a place Julianne would want to be stuck overnight. Nor would she ever want to explore the trail beyond this elevation again.

"I thought we were going to look for clues about Frederick's past?" she questioned.

"I searched the entire meadow while you were sleeping. There's nothing here of interest."

"No loose stones with hidden treasure troves beneath them?"

He hefted the day pack to his shoulder. "Not that I could find."

"Then I suppose it's back to the stuffy library and dusty journals for us?" She sighed. "And trying to figure out why Frederick had such an interest in toads." At least all of that effort could be accomplished with her feet planted solidly on terra firma. She felt like such a fool letting her fear of heights get to her. Particularly in front of Erich.

"I'm afraid that's what we're up against." He motioned for her to lead the way down the pleasantly wide path to where they had parked the car. "I do need to stop in the village on our way home. My sister asked me to pick up a prescription at the pharmacy for her."

"No problem."

As the sun settled slowly behind alpine peaks, they drove the short distance to the village. Parking on the outskirts, they walked along cobblestone streets reserved for pedestrians. Just as they were about to enter the pharmacy, which was in the center of the village, a narrow-faced man with weathered features approached them.

"Consort of warlocks!" the old man shouted, shaking a gnarled finger at Julianne. "May your flesh feel the lick of flame and your soul wither in Hades!"

Chapter Seven

Julianne blanched under the old man's verbal assault.

"Hans! That's enough!" Erich quickly stepped to Julianne's side and placed his hand at the small of her back in a possessive, protective gesture. A muscle rippling in his jaw, he radiated tension and fury barely held in check.

"And you, Erich Langlois, spawn of that same warlock, are at fault for leading this woman from a righteous path!" The old man shook his fist at them both.

"Witches and warlocks a-aren't r-real," Julianne finally sputtered.

Her accuser's brown eyes narrowed. "We know what you are up to, traitor to the Berker name."

She bristled. "Who told you a thing like that?"

"There are no secrets in Lohr am See. By your actions, your own grandmother may be thrown from her home. Discarded like so much trash. How do you justify consorting with a man who would see your own flesh and blood left to die homeless and alone on our cold, icy streets?"

"Get away from us," Erich ordered in a low, menacing voice.

Not wanting Erich to fight her battles for her, Julianne told the old man, "I think you're exaggerating." She refused to back away, in spite of the fact that for an old guy he was downright intimidating and looked as strong as a whip. His eyes glowed with the conviction of a zealot.

A man wearing a priest's frock stepped into the fray. "Hans, this young woman is a guest in our village. You must not frighten her."

"Get him out of here," Erich muttered under his breath to the priest.

"We have to beware of curses—" The old man clutched at the silver cross dangling from his neck. His gaze darted frantically around the village square.

"That is my job, Hans," the priest said in a calm voice designed to reassure penitents. "You must go back to your museum. It is almost closing time."

The words blunted Hans's attack. "Yes. Yes, of course. But you will see that—"

"You have my word," the priest vowed. Looping his arm around Hans's shoulders, he turned the old man toward the ancient stone building that housed the museum. "You may leave all of this in the hands of the Lord."

Julianne exhaled a grateful sigh when the museum keeper disappeared out of sight beyond the tower building. How had Erich withstood the mean-spirited ugliness of the villagers all these years? The ugliness that had driven his mother away?

"Peter, you've got to put a muzzle on that old man," Erich said to the priest. "He's started to believe he really is Krampas, even without his costume."

"I know. He's very excitable."

A group of curious villagers had gathered around them. Lifting her chin, Julianne produced her most persuasive smile, one she used to sway irate customers to her point of view. No way was she going to let some nut intimidate her. Or influence the local villagers who didn't know what she was up to, or why.

A younger man shoved his way through the crowd. "What's going on here?" he asked. Dressed in a conservative blue suit and equally dull tie, he looked to Julianne like a junior executive with little imagination and an equally limited future.

"Julianne, this is Paul Werndl," Erich said by way of a rather curt introduction. "We can handle things, Paul."

The new arrival bowed formally to Julianne, all but clicking his heels together. "Erich's sister Helene has told me you have been visiting our small village. I can only wish your welcome had been more courteous."

Julianne immediately realized this was the boyfriend who'd been applying pressure to have the Langlois name cleared, and holding out on wedding plans until it was. Not very tall, his shoulders appeared narrow in spite of the unusually thick shoulder pads in his suit. His face was equally thin and swallow-looking. Hardly the kind of man a girl would swoon over, Julianne mused. But maybe Helene didn't have all that many choices in this closed community.

"Until Hans came after me, I'd felt quite welcome," she said.

"I tend to attract negative attention," Erich admitted, his anger still palpable in the tautness of his tone. "I'm sorry you were caught up in the insanity."

"It's all right." She tried to shrug off the attack as meaningless, but inside she was still shaken.

"This incident clearly demonstrates," Paul extorted, "the importance of your efforts to clear the Langlois name. Helene should not be made to suffer one day longer. Not one minute more than she has already."

Erich glowered at Paul. "Let *me* worry about my sister."

As the tension crackled between the two men, the priest placed a restraining hand on Erich's arm. "Sometimes digging into the past only brings greater pain to people in the present. None of us would want any harm to come to Frau Berker."

Whipping his angry gaze toward the priest, Erich said, "But the Langlois don't matter? A false accusation made a hundred and fifty years ago still carries weight? Is that what you mean, Father?"

"I did not mean—"

"Come on, Erich." Julianne slid her arm through his. She wanted to diffuse the animosity radiating from the gawking villagers, as well as the subtle disapproval of the priest, and the best way to do that was to get the heck out of the village square. While Paul Werndl might give her a creepy feeling, at least he shared Erich's concern for his sister. She'd give him a few points for that.

"Let's get the prescription you need and go on home," she told Erich. "The Sisters will be wondering what's taking us so long."

Erich scanned the square with a look that lowered his brows into a grim line, then nodded. "Very well," he said abruptly, turning toward the pharmacy.

They didn't receive a much warmer welcome inside the small store than they had in the square, and were treated with quiet efficiency without a single smile. The guy behind the counter wasn't exactly your friendly neighborhood pharmacist, Julianne concluded as he handed over the filled prescription.

"Who do you think has been talking about what we've been up to at Schloss Lohr?" Julianne asked Erich as they left the store.

He held open the door for her. "The Sisters aren't exactly noted for keeping quiet about anything. Perhaps they've been talking around the village."

Julianne supposed that was all too possible. Even probable. Though she searched her memory for who else might know about the Langlois journals. In some ways, it hardly seemed possible Grandma Erna would be spreading the word that she might have no legitimate claim to the castle.

In the few minutes Erich and Julianne had spent inside the small store, the crowd in the village square had dispersed. There was no sign of Paul or the priest, either.

"I got the impression during that flap with Hans that you're not exactly fond of your would-be brother-in-law," she commented.

"*Not exactly* is an understatement. There's something about Paul that truly grates on me. But Helene claims she's in love with the man, though I certainly can't see why."

Neither did Julianne, her taste apparently running more toward a man with dark hair, intense blue eyes and broad shoulders, who wouldn't be any more suitable for her than Paul was for Helene. She sighed. "Maybe you're simply being an overprotective big brother?"

"Possibly," he conceded, though he didn't sound convinced.

As they walked through the village square, Julianne rotated her head to ease the tension tugging at her shoulder blades.

"I think what we have here with the villagers is a problem of image," she told Erich. As twilight approached someone had turned a spotlight on the church steeple, which would make the structure visible throughout the entire valley. Definitely an imposing sight, one that would cause a real witch to quake in her boots.

"Image?"

"Sure. The villagers are always seeing you glowering at them—"

"Like a fire-breathing dragon?"

"You got it. It seems to me, even if you clear Frederick's name of the witchcraft thing, the villagers aren't going to leap all over themselves trying to be friends."

"I've never felt I needed their friendship."

"See? There you go, being a grumpy ol' dragon again. You weren't like that with the kids at the playground."

"I wasn't?" His lips did that seductive little twitch that suggested a smile and made Julianne's heart take a tumble in the process. "Here in the village I've had more than thirty years to perfect the art of being a dragon. Or, if you'd prefer, an evil warlock."

"That may be fine for you, but your grumpy reputation is washing up on my shore. I don't exactly appreciate having misguided old men accuse me of consorting with warlocks." Consorting with a dragon in search of a willing virgin might be a different matter altogether.

"I've apologized for that."

"It wasn't your fault and no apology is necessary. The problem is your attitude. The villagers are ready to believe awful things about you because you've kept your distance from them your whole life. They haven't had a chance to get to know you." They hadn't seen, as Julianne had, Erich's wit, his love of the Alps, or the careful way he could form bread dough. Or learned to value his devotion to his sister. Or how he had a basic love for teaching children about his dreams. How could they when he hadn't given them a chance?

"The problem is that I am a *Langlois*. The villagers don't *want* to get to know either me or my sister."

"I remember a girl in my seventh-grade class who just plain hated me and for no reason that I could see. So I made it a point to say hello to her every day. If she was wearing a nice blouse or something, I'd compliment her. After a while—"

"The Langlois have been ostracized for more than a century. I doubt a few compliments will change how the villagers feel about us."

Julianne thought Erich had it wrong. In her experience, a smile and a pleasant word or two went a long way toward making friends. At least in Erich's case, she was sure not a woman in the world would be able to resist the dazzling smile he was so parsimonious about bestowing.

"Look, I'm going to the beer gardens tonight and undo any damage that incident with Hans did to my reputation," she said. "I think you ought to come, too."

He eyed her speculatively. "I understood from your comments at Schloss Lohr that you did not wish to go dancing with me."

"Well, I—I didn't mean we had to go together." She mentally backpedaled. Lord, how had she maneuvered herself into this kind of a corner? "I wasn't asking you out, or anything like that."

His eyes sparked with blatant male ego at the white lie she'd told. "In that case, Julianna, I would be honoręd if you would accompany me this evening to the Boar's Head Pub."

"YOU MUST WEAR something lovely." Olga sorted through the small selection of clothing hanging in Julianne's armoire.

"Something irresistible," Erna agreed.

"We're just going to the pub in the village," Julianne protested. "Besides, I only packed a couple of dresses. My jeans will be fine."

"Oh, no, dear. A man likes to see a woman's legs. They find them quite thrilling."

"I don't think Erich is that easily thrilled, Grandmother."

Olga produced one of Julianne's two dresses from the closet, a summery print with spaghetti straps. "This will do nicely."

Fingering the full, cotton skirt, Erna announced her decision. "Perfect!"

"I'm sure most of the singles will be dressed very informally. Jeans and T-shirts probably." In Julianne's case, she wasn't eager to reveal too much bare skin in Erich's presence. She'd consider a cloth sack if one were available. Canceling the date sounded like an even wiser decision. She didn't want to repeat the temptation of the kiss they'd shared in the meadow. With his obsession about Frederick and the ownership of Schloss Lohr, Erich just wasn't the kind of man she could trust.

If it hadn't been for Hans attacking her in the village, she never would have gotten herself into this mess.

"Oh, my," Erna exclaimed. She pulled a plastic garment bag from the back of the closet. "I had meant to show you this when you first arrived. In all the excitement, I forgot."

"What is it, Grandmother?"

Erna hung the bag from the top of the armoire door, then lifted the bottom to reveal the dress inside.

Julianne's breath caught. "Mother's wedding dress!"

Smiling sadly, Erna said, "She was such a pretty bride. I remember..." Reverently, she touched the row of satin rosettes that decorated the lace bodice. "I made this, you know. I had always hoped..."

Tears appeared in Erna's eyes, and Julianne felt the sting of her own emotion echoing her grandmother's grief.

"Sister has been wondering if you would like to take the dress back with you to America," Olga added when Erna seemed too emotional to speak. "Then, when you marry..."

"Oh, Grandma, I'd love to." Julianne's chest filled with love for both of the Sisters, and in some way that eased the loss she felt in her mother's death. "Not that there's any man in sight who'd be interested in marrying me." Quite the opposite, in fact.

"There will be, dear," Erna assured her, patting her cheek affectionately. "Perhaps sooner than you think."

"Much sooner," Olga agreed.

"Now then..." Erna seemed to gather herself. "Since we have decided what you will wear tonight, I really must see to Frederick. He has been napping most of the day."

Julianne did a mental double take. "Ghosts take naps?"

"Well, of course, dear. Frederick is getting on in years, you know."

Olga giggled. "I hope he does not hear you saying that. He thinks of himself as quite robust."

Erna ignored her niece's comment, though a sweep of color tinged her cheeks. "And while I am sure he is quite pleased to have you visiting the castle, and Erich taking such a fine interest in all of his journals, he does find having guests in the house very tiring."

Why did that sound so reasonable coming from her grandmother, Julianne wondered, when there wasn't a lick of sense in ghosts having to take naps? Or in ghosts at all, she reminded herself with a troubled shake of her head.

THE MOMENT Julianne and Erich walked into the pub the room went silent, as if someone had pressed the mute button on a television or the earth had stopped spinning on its axis for a fractional beat. Then the buzz of conversation began again, building slowly to a crescendo as pub-goers moved aside to make a path for the new arrivals. No one smiled. No one extended a warm greeting or offered a handshake.

The reality of Erich's total isolation within this small community made Julianne sick to her stomach and raised the hackles on the back of her neck. The fact that some of the animosity was newly directed toward her was almost as troubling.

As instinctively as she might have leapt to the defense of child being bullied, she linked her arm through Erich's and searched the room for a familiar face. Through a cloud of cigarette smoke, she spotted the salesclerk from the bakery where she'd made almost daily purchases with the Sisters.

"Hi, Ingrid," she called, waving across the room. "Your strudel was delicious today."

The young woman's returning smile was tentative, as was her nod of thanks.

"Hope your baby is feeling better now," Julianne added.

"*Ja*, much better, thank you," she responded with considerably more warmth.

Julianne proceeded to dazzle anyone who would meet her gaze with her very best smile. She'd chosen a career that required a great deal of public contact because she loved people. With few exceptions, they loved her back. She intended for some of that feeling to spill over onto the man whose arm she clung to so tightly, and to ease any lingering doubts about her own motives. In fact, in the time she'd been in Lohr am See, she'd felt an amazingly kindred spirit with the villagers, something she attributed to the strong Austrian genes her mother had passed on to her.

Now she made a special point to let that feeling show.

One by one the customers in the pub accepted her message of friendship.

Erich led them to a table off to the side of the room, out of the direct line of vision of most of the customers and not too close to the musicians who were returning to their places on the risers. With a signal to the bartender, he ordered two beers.

"How did you do that?" he asked, admiring the way Julianne had handled herself in an awkward situation. He'd walked through acrimonious crowds like that before. The fact that Julianne had done it with such ease amazed him. That she had done it with her hand on his arm was oddly gratifying.

"Do what?"

"In two seconds you had everyone in the room eating out of your hand."

"I told you, a smile works wonders."

"But you've only been in town a week or so. How did you even know Ingrid's child has been ill?" Erich had probably spoken to the young woman at the bakery a thousand times in the last few years and had no idea she was even married.

"Oh, women talk about things like that." Julianne lifted her delicate shoulders in an easy shrug, accenting creamy smooth shoulders that tempted a man to touch, to caress. "All you have to do is pay attention. I remember one guest we had staying at the hotel—now, she was a real witch, giving all of our staff a hard time about clean towels and room service, stuff like that. I just happened to overhear her talking to someone about her elderly father, who was sick in the hospital there in town. So every day I made it a point to ask how he was doing. She started tipping so well the room service staff was fighting over who would deliver her breakfast. She'd just been worried . . .''

His eyes narrowed in a teasing accusation. "Ah, eavesdropping is your secret of success."

She had the good grace to blush. "It doesn't hurt. But the smile is what gets them. And really caring about what goes on in their lives, of course."

"You *do* care, don't you?" Even about a roomful of mostly strangers who that very afternoon had been ready to condemn her for associating with a Langlois.

"Sure. When you get right down to it, this is a pretty small planet we live on." She leaned forward, her low-cut dress giving Erich an enticing view of the swell of her breasts. "Why don't you try a smile on the waitress when she brings our beer? You know, one like you give the kids in your climbing class."

Erich frowned. The waitress was married to one of the tenant farmers who worked a Berker leasehold, property that should rightfully belong to the Langlois. He doubted he'd have much in common with her, but knew unpredictable rains had made times financially difficult for the farmers in recent years. Her need for a little extra cash was no doubt why she was working in the pub.

"Go ahead," Julianne urged again in a conspiratorial whisper. "You have a very nice smile. Almost as nice as your knees."

He felt the corners of his mouth twitch in response to her comment just as the waitress arrived. Julianne's timing was impeccable.

Looking up at the dour-faced woman, he said, "Good evening, Anna. I imagine you and your husband are hoping the rains behave themselves this season."

Giving him an odd look, the waitress almost dropped her tray before returning his smile with a tentative one of her own. "*Ach, ja*, last year was not good." She set the bottles and glasses on the small table. "Is there anything else I can get you, Herr Langlois?"

"Some peanuts would be nice. Or pretzels. When you have a chance."

"Of course." Her smile was far warmer as she went off to fetch his order.

"See? What'd I tell you?" Julianne poured beer into her glass, wondering if her strategy had just backfired. Naturally she didn't mind if a young, sexy thing with huge boobs and bleached-blond hair had all but glowed when Erich bestowed his smile on her—particularly since she was married. Julianne didn't have a jealous bone in her body. Or, at least, she had never experienced the sharp slice of that particular two-edged sword before. It was definitely a sensation she intended to ignore.

Erich Langlois, after all, might still wrest control of Schloss Lohr from her grandmother. In spite of the fact she'd practically forced the man to invite her out this evening, she had no intention of letting matters go any

further. Indeed, she'd be back on a plane to Minneapolis within a few short weeks. She was not, definitely
not going to let her heart get involved. A kiss or two was
the limit of her involvement. No big deal, she assured
herself.

Searching for a neutral topic, Julianne said, "We
should have thought to invite Helene and her boyfriend along tonight. Your sister's a lovely young
woman." And would have provided an adequate chaperon.

"Lovely?" He looked surprised by her comment.

"I've always envied stately women. They can carry
off panache so easily while I'm stuck with being nothing but average."

Lifting his beer glass, his eyes narrowed and he gave
her a mock salute. "That's not how I've thought of
her... or you."

How did he think of her? Julianne wondered, her insides churning at the husky warmth of his voice. Maybe
she'd be better off not knowing.

The combo started its first number after the break,
the amplified music bouncing off the rustic stone walls
and tumbling back from the high-beamed ceiling to re-
verberate around the pub.

Erich stood and extended his hand. "Shall we?"

Looking up at him, Julianne had a sinking feeling she
was about to compound her problems. Dressed once
again in unrelenting black, his turtleneck sweater
stretched to encompass his broad shoulders, narrowed
into his lean waist and pulled tautly across a ribbed

belly. His dark slacks hugged the hips and muscular thighs of an athlete. If he danced as good as he looked, she was a goner. Because, unlike climbing to perilous heights, dancing was one of her all time favorite things to do, finding the perfect partner, a lifetime goal.

She sighed and placed her hand in his. *Please let him be a klutz on the dance floor,* she prayed.

Within minutes she realized her prayer had fallen on deaf ears. Erich was a dynamite dancer. Agile. Graceful in a masculine way. A perfect sense of rhythm. And easy to follow.

She watched him move to the frenzied beat of a rock classic, hips swaying, pelvis pumping, his powerful body flexing, and she echoed his gyrations. Although they weren't touching, she felt his heat. In her most private places her body responded to his tempting pantomime of love-making. She wanted him. Accepted him. Felt her body open for his penetration as if the sensation were real.

Her breath came in quick little pants; sweat trickled down the side of her face and between her breasts.

The combo segued into a slower number, giving the dancers a respite from the wild pace.

Snaring her, Erich looped his arms around her waist and pulled her close. She reciprocated by linking her hands behind his neck, threading her fingers through the dark, damp hair at his nape. Like silk, she thought, fine strands that encircled her fingers as surely as he was weaving a web around her heart.

Thigh to thigh, pelvis to pelvis, they moved in sensual heat. The dim lighting in the pub and the crowded dance floor hid the arousal that she could feel all too keenly pressing against her abdomen.

This is the wrong man, she thought in a brief effort to save her sanity before she gave herself over to the heat and need that were consuming her.

And to the inevitability of what was sure to follow.

Chapter Eight

He couldn't do this.

Dancing with Julianne was like free climbing a vertical cliff without safety ropes or an anchor. Only a fool took that kind of a risk.

His palm rested on the swell of her hip, and he ached to let his hand slip lower where he could feel the softness of her flesh. Her floral scent made his senses reel. Never in his life had he wanted a woman like this, with a desperation that brought questions to mind about his good judgment.

A deep, anguished sound vibrated through his chest as unfamiliar hunger knotted in his gut and claws of fire raked at his good reason.

He could not, *dared not*, lose track of the fact that Julianne was a Berker, a descendant of the man who had betrayed the Langlois. And he, Erich Langlois, had vowed to set matters straight. Never had he been so much at the mercy of his treasonous body as he had been since Julianne had arrived in Lohr am See. Even now, when he sought for control, the press of her breasts against his chest was a sweet torment of denial. Her every movement a painful lash designed in a special hell to diminish his good reason.

If he tried to claim the prize he so eagerly desired—Julianne in his bed—he'd be deluding himself about the eventual price they might both have to pay.

Dimly he became aware of excited conversation in the pub, the dancers halting midbeat, and the quieting of one instrument in the combo after the other until the music stopped entirely.

"What's happening?" Julianne asked. Cheeks flushed, she slowly released her linked hands from around his neck. Her breasts rose and fell in a cadence far more arousing than the music had been.

"I'm not sure." He dragged his gaze away from her to sweep around the pub. The local police chief was in animated conversation with a couple of young men, known to Erich as fellow climbers and occasional guides. From bits and pieces of the conversation, he gathered someone was in trouble. "It sounds as if a hiker has fallen somewhere on the Kitzsteinhorn, a major peak to the south of us, and his partner just returned to the village to report the problem. They're putting together a rescue team."

"Now? In the middle of the night?"

"They'll leave before dawn and be ready to climb at first light."

She sighed, rested her head on his shoulder, and he felt a silent shudder ripple through her slender body. "You'll be careful, won't you?"

"Careful?"

"You're going with them, aren't you?"

"No."

Her head snapped up at his tone. "Why on earth not? You're the best climber around, aren't you? It seems to me they'd need everybody they could find if some poor guy is in trouble."

"Have you forgotten? I'm a Langlois."

"Phooey! What does that have to do with anything if you could help to save the man's life? You can bet his family wouldn't care if you were Dracula himself."

His lips twitched. "You're a very determined young lady."

"Well, at least offer to help. If they turn you down . . ." She shrugged. "You'll know you tried, anyway. And maybe they'll stop thinking of you as such a rotten ogre."

Perhaps she was right, he mused. Erich had occasionally wondered who would assist him should he get into difficulties in the mountains. It might be just as well if he offered his services, even if they were rejected because of the villagers' narrow-minded attitudes.

She gave him a little nudge. "The worst they can say is no," she reminded him.

He made his way through the crowd, Julianne at his side.

"What is it, Viktor?" he asked the man seated at the table.

The younger's man surprised gaze rose to meet his. "A boy has fallen from the outside edge of Gustav's Face and is wedged in the lower chimney."

"Is he alive?"

"His friend thinks so, but that was hours ago." He lifted his muscular shoulders in a resigned shrug. "I do not see how we can get him out of there. No one has successfully climbed Gustav's Face."

"I have," Erich said. From the circle of men surrounding the table, Erich sensed both skepticism and animosity. "With the right partner, the climb is possible. Retrieving an injured climber, however, will make it much more difficult. We would need to approach from above, taking a line to the headwall, then lower him to another team, who would wait at the rock ledge."

There was a murmur of agreement among the men.

Viktor scrutinized Erich with considerable care. "Are you willing to try?"

"If you are," he agreed, acknowledging that Viktor would be a suitable partner for the ascent and rescue, and challenging him at the same time.

Viktor shoved back his chair. "Done." He extended his hand. "We'll meet at road's end at five and begin at first light. Meanwhile, I will arrange our backup teams."

Julianne listened while Erich made his plans with Viktor, wondering if she should have kept her mouth shut. The thought of Erich dangling from a rope while Viktor swung him over a ledge like a human pendulum sent a chill down her spine, and her palms began to sweat. In her view, a person who climbed mountains for a living had to be just a little bit crazy.

Finally, Erich turned to her. "I'm afraid this means I must take you home now. I'll have to gather my gear and catch a few hours of sleep if I am to be ready on time."

"I understand." In fact, it was better the evening had ended this way rather than how she had anticipated its conclusion only minutes ago. In her mind she had already made love with Erich and was waiting only for the moment of reality to arrive. She'd been eager. Perhaps too eager.

It was much better she'd been given a reprieve to consider all the consequences of such an act.

Sure it was, she chided herself for the liar she was. She'd escaped capture by the dragon this time. Perversely, she wasn't at all happy about it.

HIS MOOD TENSE, Erich strode from where he'd parked the car toward his house. While intellectually he knew the change in plans had saved him from making a huge mistake, his body had not gotten the message. He wanted to go back to Schloss Lohr, slip into the secret passage, and climb up the hidden stairway to Julianne's room. Then he would do as he had been tempted to do so many times. He'd make love to her until dawn, until he had learned the secret of why she aroused him more than any other woman had.

He gritted his teeth against a renewed surge of desire. She'd feel so damn good in his arms; he'd feel so damn good buried inside her flesh.

He shoved open the back door. Unconcerned that Helene might be asleep, he marched into the dark house and didn't switch on the light until he reached the living room.

A little cry came from the couch, matched by a male voice muttering a curse. Two people scrambled to their feet.

"Erich, I didn't expect you home so soon." Breathless, Helene turned her back and furiously began straightening her blouse and skirt. "Paul and I were just—"

"I know what you were doing," Erich said roughly. He glared at the couple.

"Good evening." Showing not the least remorse for having been caught in a compromising situation, Paul tucked in his shirt. "We assumed your evening at the pub would last much longer."

"Obviously." A muscle ticked in Erich's jaw. He was furious Paul was trying to take advantage of his sister right in his own house.

"We weren't doing anything wrong," Helene said defensively, her lower lip forming a petulant pout. With a sweep of her fingers she tried to smooth the tangles from her long, dark hair.

Erich studied his sister with new appreciation and considerable apprehension. Julianne had said Helene was lovely, and she'd been right. Though still young, his sister had the makings of a beautiful woman. He wondered why he hadn't noticed before.

She shouldn't, he realized, be limited in her choices to men like Paul Werndl, a man he instinctively disliked though he couldn't quite pinpoint the reason why.

"I suggest you tell Paul good-night," he told his sister abruptly. The need to clear the Langlois name as soon as possible weighed heavily on Erich's conscience as he headed for his workroom to gather his gear for the morning. Somehow he had to find a way to explain the troubling concoctions noted in Frederick's journals.

But in no way did his concerns reduce his irrational need to possess Julianne, to make her his own...in spite of all the reasons, he shouldn't even be considering the possibility.

JULIANNE LOITERED in the village square the better part of the next day. She turned eavesdropping into a fine art. When that failed, she butted her way into any conversation she could find that might shed some light on what was happening on the far-off mountain peak where Erich was risking his life.

Rumors sped around the square like miniature whirlwinds. Contradictory reports drove her crazy. No one seemed to be sure what was happening.

As the afternoon slid toward evening, a storm approached and dark rain clouds streamed like smoke between two lushly forested hillsides to the west. The temperature dropped precipitously, suggesting the possibility of snow at the higher elevations. She could only hope the rescue party would be down off the mountain before the storm enveloped them and created even greater dangers for the work they had to do.

Her own fear of heights got tangled with a new and equally frightening set of emotions—feelings she had for Erich that made her as dizzy as if she were leaning over a precipice. The entire ordeal took her breath away.

When the first drops of rain spattered onto the cobblestones of Lohr am See, she decided to go back to the castle. It wouldn't do anyone any good if she caught pneumonia. And surely she could worry just as effectively within the confines of Schloss Lohr as she could on the village square.

"But you must eat something," Olga insisted at the dinner table that evening.

"I'm sorry." Julianne shoved her untouched food away. "I know it's delicious, but I simply don't have any appetite."

Erna patted her hand. "Erich will be fine," she assured her granddaughter. "You'll see."

Julianne's chin trembled. "I think I'll go take a look at one of Frederick's journals. It will keep my mind off what's happening."

"Of course, dear. We will leave the door unlatched for Erich in case he decides to drop by later."

"Thank you," she said softly, automatically.

In truth, Julianne wanted to be in the library where she'd spent so much time with Erich. Somehow it made her feel closer to him, as though she could still catch his leather and spice scent, still remember the tactile sensation of being in his arms while they danced, the warmth of his lips on hers.

She lit a fire against the evening's chill and settled down on the couch to begin her reading. But she couldn't concentrate. Not on toad stew, or why names of villagers appeared to be listed below the ingredients. Or why any of this would trigger some distant memory she couldn't quite latch on to.

She wanted Erich there, with her, not stranded on some cliff in the dark with pouring rain or snow making his tenuous holds even more precarious.

Her focus faltered as her eyes filled with tears. The scrawled words on the page swam until they were no longer legible.

Please don't let anything bad happen to him.

At the sound of the lock on the library door snicking open, Julianne's head snapped up.

He materialized out of the shadows, the door locked behind him in guarantee of privacy. Firelight painted him with an evocative brush of light and darkness. Grim lines of fatigue etched his face. His shirt was dirt-streaked and stained with sweat, his pants scored by jagged rocks. As he walked across the room, Julianne's heartbeat accelerated.

"Erich..." she said on an anxious sigh.

She went to him, instinctively wrapping him in her arms, resting her head against his broad shoulder, reassuring herself Erich was safe. His icy shirt smelled of fresh snow and the sweat of exertion. As she hugged him tightly and sent up a small prayer of thanksgiving, he trembled.

"Are you all right?" she asked.

"I'm fine." His raspy voice spoke of the hours of exertion he'd undergone.

"The boy who fell? Is he..."

"We got him off the mountain safely but he's in pretty bad shape. The doctors don't know if he will make it or not."

"Oh, no..."

"I thought about waiting till morning to let you know, but I wanted—"

"I'm glad you came now. I was going crazy worrying about you." She palmed his jaw, cherishing the rough texture of his evening whiskers.

He studied her with eyes filled with a keen intensity. "No one has worried about me since I was a child."

His admission tightened like a band around Julianne's heart. He'd been deprived for most of his life of the love and affection she had taken for granted. She wanted to make up for every slight he had experienced, fill his empty glass to overflowing if she could.

Holding his face between her palms, she rose on tiptoe. "Worrying is one of my top skills," she whispered against his lips.

At her invitation he claimed her mouth in a hungry kiss that sent sensuous flames of fire licking from her breasts to her midsection, stealing her breath. His tongue probed in an exploration of the peaks and valleys he found, territory more sensitive than she had ever imagined possible. His palm caressed the frantic pulse point on her neck.

The barely controlled fear she'd felt for Erich's safety tumbled into an avalanche of sexual need. Adrenaline flowed through her bloodstream and fired her desire. She had never been more aware. Aware of herself—the heat building in her body, the dampness forming between her thighs, the increasing slickness of her skin. Even her clothing seemed suddenly too tight, the lace of her bra cutting into her tender flesh.

She tasted sugared coffee on his tongue, felt flaming heat where his chest pressed against her breasts, experienced the need to be closer still and naked in his arms.

As though he could read her mind, Erich urged her across the room, to the fireplace with its flickering golden light. Tugging a crocheted afghan from the back of the couch, he spread it on the floor in front of the hearth.

In his taut movements, she sensed residual tension fed by the danger he had survived.

"Julianna, my sweet, beautiful worrier..."

His hands spanned her midriff, pulling her shirt from her waistband, touching her bare skin with his fingertips, teasing the underside of her breasts as he lifted the soft fabric over her head.

A low moan escaped her throat as cool air chilled her overheated flesh. She shivered.

The clock on the mantel struck the witching hour, reminding Julianne she was in Schloss Lohr with the man who wanted to claim the castle as his own.

"Erich, I can't," she protested, her legs trembling wildly, her mind just as unsteady. "You're going to take Grandma's castle from her. I can't—"

"No, Julianna. I swear, no matter what we discover, no matter what the magistrates may rule, as long as Erna and Olga live they will have a home here at Schloss Lohr. On my honor..."

She believed his promise.

How could she not when he was raining kisses on her throat, moist kisses that traveled lower until they teased at the lace edge of her bra? Her nipples tightened and strained against the fabric, begging, pleading for a chance to feel his lips, his tongue.

Giving way to the weakness in her knees, she sank to the floor, Erich sinking with her until they were both kneeling, facing each other. In a swift motion he removed his shirt, baring his finely muscled chest to her view. Hesitantly she mapped the dark, curly hair that formed an intriguing cross before the sworls vanished below the waistband of his pants. Then she tested the corded strength of his arms. He was like iron, filled with restrained power gained by climbing the highest peaks the Alps had to offer.

"You're magnificent," she whispered, a smile teasing at her lips. Not a dragon at all, she mused, but the perfect lover she had always dreamed about.

Her fingertips grazed a welt that arrowed diagonally across his chest. She raised questioning eyes.

"Falls are not uncommon on any climb. The rope leaves a mark."

Fear clawed at her throat. "You could have died!"

He shrugged, the truth evident in his dark eyes, though there was no trace of fear. "And my only regret as I hung on for dear life was that I had never made love with you. That is the reason I could not wait until the morning. I needed you now."

"No more than I need you."

The clothes they hastily shed made a sibilant sound as fabric slid along flesh. Shadows danced with equal fervor across his muscular body and her feminine curves, gilding them both in golden warmth.

The fire sighed as a puff of wind came down the chimney to swirl the flames. The magic of the moment transported Julianne to a world she'd had no idea existed, a place of intense passion, elemental yet so complex she couldn't grasp the acute pleasure of one sensation before Erich's mouth and hands taught her of new hedonistic experiences even more stunning.

When he rose above her, she arched reflexively with the thrill of pleasure and anticipation. The pain was so slight she hardly noticed, the mild discomfort replaced by joy as her body eagerly stretched to accommodate his size. He filled her, yet she wanted more.

Tension coiled nerve endings taut as he thrust into her. Once. Twice. Then again. Deeper and harder each time. She cried out and burst like a spring torrent rupturing a dam and knew in her heart she would never again be the same.

The first wave of her release closed around Erich. Struggling for control to savor the moment, he clenched his teeth. She was beautiful in the full throes of sexual arousal. Her flushed skin was like a gleaming, polished gem, but softer and far more pliable. Her hair caught the highlights from the fading fire and glowed with vitality, curving against her cheek like a lover's caress. Her eyes were dark with passion and filled with the wonder of new discovery.

He'd taken her virginity. The responsibility for that act weighed heavily on his conscience even as his masculine pride relished the knowledge that he had been her first lover.

Why such a beautiful, loving woman had waited so long to relinquish such a precious gift he didn't know. Nor did he want to find out. The knowledge would give her too much power over a foolish dragon who'd been so bold as to leave the safety and isolation of his cave.

He had not fully understood the emotional toll making love to Julianne would take. Always before he had held some piece of himself back from a woman. That was impossible with Julianne. She gave so freely, so innocently, she evoked from him the same generosity. He could only hope his momentary lapse in self-control would not result in the kind of tragedy a similar slip on a climb would cost.

She moved beneath him, shuddering again, and all further thoughts were lost as Erich ascended the highest peak he had ever experienced, then plummeted into space in an unending free-fall.

ERICH TUGGED a corner of the afghan over Julianne to keep her warm. It didn't matter. His heat was all she needed. His raging metabolism made him an ideal man to cuddle with on a cold, wintery night.

Somewhat anxiously, she waited for him to comment on her having been a virgin. A situation that was now decidedly, and quite pleasantly, past tense. But then, perhaps proper dragon etiquette didn't call for comment.

Sighing into the silence, she snuggled her head on his shoulder. "Tell me what happened on the mountain."

His hand idly stroked her upper arm. "The boy was stuck in a very narrow chimney. To get to him I had to come down an outer edge that was as smooth as glass. Viktor was well secured above me, but I needed another anchor. Because of the terrain, I was forced to offset a cam—that's a spring-loaded device a climber can lock on to. I knew it was risky..."

"But you did it anyway."

"There was no other choice if we wanted to get that boy out of there. He was only eighteen years old. Far too young and inexperienced to have tried such a technically difficult climb."

"So you risked your neck to save his."

He brushed a kiss to her forehead. "You were the one who encouraged me to volunteer my services."

"I've had a lot of time to rethink my position. Next time—"

He claimed her mouth in a quick, thrusting kiss. "Next time I'll do exactly the same thing. And hope for the same welcome from you."

Finger-combing his dark hair back from his forehead, she laughed and said, "Do I detect a hero who's just a little too sure of himself?"

"On a mountain, that attitude can be dangerous. I imagine it's the same with women."

"Absolutely." In her case, Erich could be as confident as he liked. Though she wasn't about to admit that to him. A woman needed to save some semblance of her pride when she'd just presented him with her virginity and there'd been no reciprocal commitments asked or given. "If you grovel sufficiently, I may consider unbarricading the secret door into my bedroom."

The corners of his eyes crinkled with a smile. "I'll look forward to earning free passage."

He levered himself to his feet, then pulled her up with him, wrapping her in the afghan. "I must go. The Sisters are early risers and I doubt they would approve of how we've made use of the library tonight."

"Probably not," she conceded, her conscience pricking her as she watched him get dressed. "Will you come back later?" *Will I see you again for more than simply wonderful sex?*

He eyed her carefully. "In the afternoon, I think. We both need to catch up on our rest."

Julianne held his promise in her heart after he left and she made her way upstairs to her bedroom. Though she wasn't at all sure sleep would come easily. At some point after the clouds of passion had dissipated, she'd realized Erich had promised a home to the Sisters for the rest of their lives, but he had not made any vow as to the future ownership of the castle, or the rights of the heir. Through her mother, Julianne was the first in line to inherit the castle when Grandma Erna died.

Chapter Nine

"You slept so late we were beginning to worry about you, dear."

"I'm fine, Grandma." Julianne poured herself a cup of rich, dark coffee, added cream, and carried it to the kitchen table. "Fine" wasn't really an apt description of her state of mind. "Confused" came closer to the truth. "Uncertain about the future" stated the case equally well.

"We have such good news from the village about Erich." Working at the sink, Olga was washing and removing stems from a quart box of strawberries. It looked like she was getting ready to make another of her famous tortes.

Erna slid the sugar bowl across the table toward Julianne. "Indeed the villagers are all atwitter about Erich getting that young boy down off the mountain."

"Why would they be *bitter?*" Olga asked over her shoulder. "Erich is nothing less than a hero. He almost died saving that foolish boy."

"*Twitter,* sister. I said twitter."

At the renewed thought of Erich dying, the combination of coffee and cream curdled in Julianne's stomach. "I know. He told me last night."

"Really, dear? I did not hear him arrive." *Or leave,* remained a question mark in her grandmother's gray eyes.

"It was late. We didn't want to wake you."

"That was very thoughtful of you. But we all were quite anxious about Erich and the injured young man. We would not have minded being woken with such good news."

Or providing her with a chaperon, Julianne imagined.

"Is he going to come by again today?" Erna asked.

"He said he would. Maybe this afternoon." Or tonight, up the secret stairway.

Heat flushed Julianne's face at the thought. Did the Sisters know, could they tell, she'd been changed for life by what she and Erich had done last night?

"Perhaps he will stay for supper," Olga suggested. She poured a cupful of Appel Spitz over the prepared strawberries. "I am fixing something special for dessert that I am sure he will enjoy."

Julianne stifled a laugh. It looked like they could all look forward to the most potent strawberry concoction imaginable.

She had a hard roll and some orange juice for breakfast, then spent the rest of the morning fussing in the kitchen with Olga and checking out old recipe books. Erna, her fingers flying, busied herself crocheting one of the many lap robes she donated each year to the village old folks' home.

Outside, a sky dark with dirty, cotton-ball clouds blocked the view of surrounding mountain peaks. Rain misted the lush landscape and crept over the eaves of the castle in slow motion.

Time passed in the same way.

Where was Erich? Julianne wondered. And what was he thinking?

And how should she behave when she saw him again?

Acting blasé wouldn't be easy, but maybe that's what he expected. Men, she suspected, took this whole lovemaking business far more casually than women. But Julianne knew no matter how many years she lived, she'd never forget her first time. The memory was indelibly imprinted in her mind. So were the intimate details of the man to whom she had given her virginity. She'd locked those memories in a special place in her heart.

Staring out into the gray mist, she worried her lower lip between her teeth. The possibility that she and Erich had a future together appeared cloaked in uncertainty.

So were her feelings for Erich.

Was it love she felt? Thoughts of him had consumed her since they'd first met, even when he'd been masquerading as a ghost. She admired his wit and charm, when he chose to use them. And yesterday she had been terrified for his safety.

Was that how a woman felt when she was in love?

Or was she experiencing the less lofty sensations of lust? And how on earth could she possibly tell the difference when all she wanted was to be in Erich's arms again?

Whatever was happening, she'd certainly never felt this way about any other man.

Erna's chair squeaked as she set her crocheting aside. "The poor souls at the old folks' home have such a difficult time. Whenever I make one of these lap robes, I count my blessings that I have not been forced to move in there myself."

"You're too young and spry for that," Julianne assured her.

"I am almost eighty, you know."

"Almost?" Olga questioned, her flour sifter whirring merrily. "How is it I am suddenly three years older than you are? When we were children, you were the eldest."

"Hush, sister! You do not have to tell the whole world."

Julianne laughed. "I think you're both good for a few more years, Grandma. I wouldn't worry about anyone sending you off to an old folks' home, no matter what your real age is."

Erna's cheeks flushed. "For someone who couldn't hear an avalanche coming if she was standing right under it," she muttered under her breath, "my dear sister has a big mouth. A woman has a right to keep her own counsel on matters of age."

Leaning over, Julianne kissed her grandmother. "Your secret is safe with me, Grandma," she whispered.

Mollified, the sparkle returned to Erna's eyes. "At least Frederick does not mind how old I am."

Julianne supposed that would be true for a hundred-plus-year-old ghost, though it did make her wonder who would take care of the Sisters if they drifted too far from reality.

A loud crash shook the castle walls.

Julianne jumped. "Good grief! Was that thunder?" She shot a glance out the window.

"Oh, my, I do hope Frederick has not hurt himself." Erna stood and hurried out of the kitchen.

Julianne was about to follow when she spotted Erich coming up the walk, his stride long and athletic and powerfully masculine. Her heart did a strange little somersault and any concern about her grandmother's mental stability simply fled from her mind. For the moment she had her own equilibrium to worry about.

She got to the door before he knocked.

Without thinking about playing their relationship cool, she yanked the door open, then stood there absolutely mute. Raindrops glistened on his dark hair like diamonds and slid down the yellow slicker he wore. In the depth of his blue eyes, she saw the flicker of passion recalled. She drew a quick breath as her body responded with an almost painful clenching sensation deep inside.

No way she could be casual about this man, she realized. No way at all.

"Do you intend for me to stand outside all afternoon?" he inquired. Sparks of teasing light danced in his eyes.

"I'm sorry...I..." Flustered, she opened the door wider. The hinges squeaked a plaintive sound that echoed of surrender, much like the silent cry of her heart. A crowd of convention-goers she could handle easily. But not Erich Langlois. He'd had her off-balance since the first moment they'd met.

He was too male, too intensely virile to be *handled* at all.

Stepping across the threshold, he gave her a kiss that she wanted to last forever. His rain-chilled lips burned her with a craving she could only now identify—her scorching need for him. Not just as a lover, but as the man she wanted to spend her life with.

"I hope you're not sorry about last night." His husky words were like a soothing caress across her anxious heart.

"No. Of course not."

"Good. Because neither am I." He shrugged out of his rain gear and draped the slicker over a rack by the door. "Where are the Sisters?"

"In the kitchen. Or they were a minute ago."

He slid his arm around her waist. "Then let's go into the library."

"Returning to the scene of the crime, are we?"

A deep, warm chuckle rumbled through his chest. "If you'd like."

Erich knew he'd like to do more than simply return to the scene. He'd relived the experience of making love to Julianne a dozen times in his dreams last night—or, more accurately, during the early morning hours. None of the misty images had been half as arousing as what he had actually experienced with Julianne. He was eager to revisit the real thing as soon as possible, though with the Sisters hovering nearby he assumed now would not be a good time.

Always before he'd been content with a mutual sharing of pleasure with a woman, a physical contact that was, at best, short lived. Indeed, he had considered that the *only* possibility in a relationship between a man and a woman. But his experience with Julianne had touched him in ways he did not yet fully understand.

How would he have even suspected there could be some deeper communication between two people? Certainly he had seen little of that between his parents and had been far too young to understand, in any event. In some strange way Erich felt that before last night he had been as much the virgin as Julianne.

He stepped into the library and came to an abrupt halt. Dumbfounded, his gaze swept the room. A deep sense of betrayal welled up in him, the bitter taste achingly familiar at the back of his throat. Rage he had fought to suppress rose up at the injustice that once again dogged his steps, twisting and turning like a licking flame.

"They're gone! Every one of Frederick's journals is gone!" Except for a rim of dust, the shelves that had once held the journals were entirely bare. Erich whirled on Julianne, a Berker he had momentarily allowed himself to trust. "What happened to them?"

Shaking her head, she crossed the room to stare more closely at the empty shelves as if that would somehow make the books reappear. "I have no idea. They were here last night."

"What did you do with them?" How had he been so stupid that he'd fallen for her act?

"Me?"

"Yes, you. All along you've been afraid we'd find the evidence necessary to clear Frederick's name, and in the process your precious grandmother would lose her home. I promised you that wouldn't happen."

"And I believed you. Though you didn't say squat about the rights of Grandma's heir." She returned his glare dagger for dagger. "The fact is, *you're* the one who has something to lose since we found that stupid book of recipes for witches' brew. How do I know you didn't sneak back in here last night and steal all the journals so they couldn't be shown to anyone else?"

"I wouldn't do that."

"Then what makes you think I would?" She lifted her sweet little chin in stubborn defiance.

She looked so damn innocent, yet that couldn't be true. Like all of the Berkers, she had a capacity for lying. Hadn't history taught him that? Leather-bound books didn't simply fly off the shelves by themselves.

"Maybe the Sisters know what happened," she suggested.

"Are you trying to tell me Erna or Olga hauled all those heavy journals out of here by themselves?"

"I don't know. But I sure as hell don't like getting blamed for something I didn't do."

Furious, Julianne stormed out of the library. She'd been burned before when she'd been tempted to give her heart to Jerry Wiggins at the hotel. An infatuation in high school had led to much the same result. She'd been telling herself all along not to get involved with Erich Langlois. Pity she hadn't been listening to her own good advice.

Mutual trust was a touchstone for any relationship as far as Julianne was concerned. Erich had just demonstrated he didn't trust her at all. That revelation hurt like hell.

His heavy footsteps right behind her punctuated that distrust.

Julianne shoved through the swinging door into the kitchen. Erna was back to her crocheting. Spreading whip cream on a torte now engaged Olga's attention.

"Sisters, do you have any idea what's happened to all of Frederick's journals that Erich and I have been studying?"

Erna's hands stopped their rhythmic hooking.

"Happened?" Olga looked up from her work. "Is there something wrong?"

"The journals are gone from the library. All of them."

"Oh, my..." Erna resumed her crocheting, the pace increasing with every stitch.

"Grandma, do you know something—"

"Of course she does," Erich mumbled. "She's trying to save her castle."

"Do you blame her?" Julianne chided.

"If the journals are gone," Erna said, her attention firmly on her handiwork, "maybe Frederick is trying to say he doesn't want you prying into his past." Her hands trembled slightly and she dropped a loop.

"Frederick has been dead more than a hundred years, Grandma."

Upset that her grandmother was so obsessed with a ghost, Julianne glanced up at Erich in search of understanding. His eyes had lost much of their flashing anger but he still appeared unconvinced of her innocence. Or that of the Sisters.

Shaking his head, he said, "I want to take a look around. If the journals are still in the castle, I'll find them."

"I supposed you'd like to look under my bed?" she snapped at him.

He eyed her speculatively. "Last night I could have thought of a much more interesting reason to enter your bedroom." He spoke so quietly, only she could hear his words.

"So could I," she muttered, fighting a whip-sawing pain at the back of her skull that threatened to bring tears to her eyes and snatch her reason away.

NEARLY AN HOUR LATER they found the journals neatly stacked in a corner of the very top room of the signal tower.

Breathing hard, Julianne sat down on a stone bench that was actually a part of the castle wall. "I'll guarantee Olga didn't bring those suckers up here. She would have had cardiac arrest." The three flights of stairs had been both narrow and steep, a good workout for almost anyone, particularly after they'd searched the entire rest of the castle first, starting with the wine cellar. Though she noted irritably Erich hadn't even broken a sweat.

"I admit it also seems unreasonable to assume Erna could have carried those journals up here on her own. It would have taken her dozens of trips." Lifting one of the leather-bound books, he stared thoughtfully out the slitted window.

"Does that mean you still think I'm the culprit?"

"No, that doesn't seem very likely, either."

"Thank you so much for that *marginal* vote of confidence."

Turning, he cocked an eyebrow at her sarcastic tone. What the hell did he expect? Bonbons and flowers because he finally recognized she wasn't the one who'd made off with the damn journals?

"How do you explain what has happened?" he asked.

How could any woman explain how she'd fallen in love with the wrong guy? Again!

But that wasn't the question he was asking.

"Maybe Grandma's right. Frederick doesn't want us messing with his past."

"You don't believe that."

"God, no. But then, nothing's seemed quite right since I arrived in Austria. Maybe jet lag's a permanent condition for me and nothing will make sense until I get back home again." Until she got away from Erich and the wildly vacillating feelings he created. Even now she wanted him to hold her, wanted to feel his lips on hers, experience the thrill of him filling her most secret places as they had never been filled before.

And at the same time she never wanted to see him again.

She got up to leave. "Well, you've found the journals again. I'll leave you to them."

Before she reached the door Erich caught her by the arm. "I could still use your help."

"Why? If I found something in those books that said Frederick was the biggest all-time witch in the world, you'd decide I'd forged the damn thing. So what's the point in me going cross-eyed reading the journals when you wouldn't believe one word I said?"

His hand slid slowly up her arm, his palm heating her through the thickness of her lightweight sweater. "I admit I'm not very good at trusting people, Julianne. Maybe you can understand that's been the way of things for the Langlois for a long time." A muscle in his jaw strained, as though an apology was an unfamiliar act and he couldn't quite find the right words.

She fought a tremble of sexual awareness. Of all the men she had ever met, Erich was the only one who'd made her feel so vulnerable. It frightened her to have her emotions on such a razor edge, to feel that she might fly apart if he touched her in a certain way. Or worse, if he said something that touched her heart. She was such a sucker for a sob story.

"The last time I told a lie I was five years old," she said softly. "When my mother found out, she washed my mouth out with soap. It was a lesson I never forgot."

His lips twitched. "My father had a paddle that was about four feet long. He propped it right by the fireplace. All he had to do was look at it, and I'd tell him anything he wanted to know." Some of the tension eased from his jaw as he absently stroked her arm. "It was a very persuasive weapon."

"I'm sorry." Sorry that he'd experienced pain, perhaps had even suffered at the hand of a brutal parent. But that was not, she told herself, *her* problem.

Julianne needed to step away from Erich. In spite of how much she wanted it not to be true, loving him was dangerous. He'd break a woman's heart. At the moment hers felt pretty fragile. With the wounds he carried from the past, he'd never be able to look toward the future. He'd already announced he had no plans to ever marry. Julianne needed to keep her distance. Maybe she could label him in her mental file cabinet under Vacation Fling and only bring out the memory of what they had done together when she felt particularly strong.

As though there'd been a gust of wind, the tower door swung shut. The metal latch dropped into place.

"What's going on?" Erich grabbed the door handle and tugged. When the heavy door didn't budge, he tried again. "The thing's locked!"

"But the latch is on the inside. It can't be locked."

He rattled the metal bar. It lifted as it should, but the door didn't give. "What the hell! Somebody's locked us in!"

Under other circumstances, that might have sounded like a terrific idea to Julianne. But not when she was feeling so vulnerable.

"How could anybody lock us in?" she asked reasonably. "We would have heard them coming up the stairs. Or seen them. It must have been the wind."

"I didn't feel any wind." He scowled at her, an art he'd perfected with dark brows that naturally formed a straight line. "Did you?"

"No." The hair at her nape crept to spooky attention. "Maybe the door's swollen shut with the dampness."

"And maybe crazy things happen in this castle all on their own. Or maybe they get a little help from someone we can't see."

"You think the resident ghost is responsible?" She swallowed hard.

He speared his fingers through his hair. "Right about now, that sounds like as good an explanation as any."

"I think the Sisters have had matchmaking on their minds since they invited you to dinner," she suggested as an alternative. Heat raced to her cheeks at the admission. "Maybe they wanted to give us a chance—"

"You just said we would have heard footsteps on the stairs. Olga, at least, isn't exactly light on her feet."

"True."

"So we have a choice of a wind we didn't feel, a ghost," he said in exasperation, "or two little old ladies who'd have a hard time making it up the stairs at all, never mind doing it so quietly we wouldn't hear them."

"Then it's got to be Frederick."

He rolled his eyes. "Right."

"Now wait a minute. Every time something weird has happened, it's been related to the journals. Like when the soup accidently spilled in your lap, you were talking about these old diaries—"

"That was no accident."

"And when the chair slid out from under you in the library you were saying how dismal his handwriting was."

"The ghost of Schloss Lohr, and Krampas, are folktales in the Alps just like the story of the Saltzburg dragon."

Their eyes met, the fairy tale of a dragon and his virgin seemed real as intimate memories heated Julianne's cheeks and warmed her most private places—those erotic places Erich had touched and kissed and caressed until she had begged him to stop and prayed that he wouldn't.

With an effort she forced herself to continue her line of reasoning.

"Maybe you're right. But the fact is, the first couple of days I was here I saw some guy who was dressed in lederhosen—"

"That was me."

"No, the man I saw had knobby knees and spindly legs. Definitely not you. At least, a couple of times he was someone else."

Erich looked at her as if she'd totally lost her mind. Which was, she realized, entirely possible.

"Look, what if the man I saw wasn't a ghost at all, but someone who knew about the secret passages through the castle just like you did? What if he is masquerading as a ghost so he can have the run of the place? Or because he's got this thing for Grandma Erna?"

"She's at least eighty years old, for heaven's sake. Why would some man—"

"Because he's eighty, too, or thereabouts. She's a very attractive woman for her age. Why shouldn't she have a boyfriend? Or even lover?"

"Good God..." He paced across the room to stand by the window. "If that's true, why would this man—whoever he is—try to prevent us from clearing Frederick's name?"

"Maybe because Grandma's sense of morality allows him to do what he wants as long as she thinks he's a ghost? She *is* just a bit dotty, you know. Or maybe because you'd take over the castle, given half a chance, and leave him out in the cold. Who knows?'' She shrugged, hugging herself against the cool, damp air coming in through the slotted windows. The openings were narrower than the breadth of a man's shoulders, but they offered little protection against the chilly weather. ''There could be any number of reasons for a man to masquerade as a ghost. Including *your* reason for sneaking into my bedroom in search of dusty old journals,'' she observed pointedly. ''I know it's a bit bizarre, but what other explanation do we have?''

''None,'' he conceded. ''Though I still don't see how Erna having a lover would explain the soup.''

''Neither do I. Not really. But neither one of us can believe in a ghost, either.''

''Okay, so we've been locked in the tower room by persons or ghosts unknown. What do we do now? We can't stay up here forever.''

As a matter of fact, Julianne could think of a whole slew of fascinating activities they could entertain themselves with, most of them strikingly similar to what she had enjoyed last evening. But she thought she ought not to mention her ideas, more for her sake than Erich's. Clearly she was already in too deep an emotional quagmire to risk further intimacy with a man who was so stingy about giving his trust.

''Well, I know what I'm going to do.'' She crossed her arms, grabbed the hem of her sweater and yanked it off over her head.

Erich nearly choked and his body instantly reacted to her unexpected, *uninhibited* striptease. "Julianne, I don't think we should—"

She looked at him blankly.

"I mean, do you really think we ought to—" Little more than a narrow strip of black lace covered her breasts and the cold had already puckered her nipples. The enticing sight had his groin aching and his fingers itching to explore the fascinating territory he'd visited the night before. He began to sweat.

Cocking her head, she said, "I'm going to yell like crazy and wave my sweater out the window. Maybe I can attract somebody's attention." She frowned. "What did you think I was going to do?"

"I, uh..." The air went out of his lungs. Didn't she know what she'd done? What effect she had on him? He'd been thinking about doing all kinds of interesting, sensual things in this tiny tower room. Obviously her thoughts were on escaping.

A wise woman, he concluded, ordering his reactions back under control.

Looking out the window, he realized the overcast sky would bring darkness early. The misting rain had driven most people inside. Even the cows that normally grazed in the various hillside pastures nearby had sought the shelter of trees and were out of sight. It was unlikely anyone would see or hear their signal, no matter how loudly Julianne shouted.

He reached outside and tested the stone construction.

"Put your sweater back on. I'll get you out of here. It shouldn't take me long."

"Not take long? What are you going to do? Dematerialize and pop up on the other side of the door? Or do you know of a secret passage you haven't told me about?"

"I'm going to climb down the tower wall."

Her jaw went slack. "You can't do that! It must be a hundred feet to the ground."

"A little less than that, I'd estimate."

"You'll kill yourself!"

"Climbing is what I do, Julianne. This particular descent is easier than most." And it would be much safer for him in the long run if he escaped temptation while he could.

"What about a rope? You can't go down Spider-Man style."

"Free-soloing isn't all that difficult if you're careful. And experienced." He unlaced his walking boots and slipped them off, along with his socks. Normally he wore shoes with flexible soles for rock climbing, but as a child he'd often gone barefoot.

"You won't even be able to get through the window," she protested even as she tugged her sweater back on over her head. "Your shoulders are too broad."

He smiled slightly. It rather pleased him she had noticed. "Sideways I'll fit fine." He hefted himself to the window ledge, paused, then eased his shoulders through the opening.

He hadn't lied to Julianne. On a relative scale, this descent was fairly simple. There were plenty of finger and toe tip pockets where the stones had been mortared in place. But free-soloing even on a practice wall took concentration and when the stones were slick with moisture, the crucial need to find solid placement for hands and feet increased exponentially. Settling his weight on an outcropping of rotten mortar could prove fatal.

JULIANNE COULDN'T watch.

The more she squeezed herself out the window to peer over the ledge, the more fearful she became. He moved so slowly, with such enormous caution, it was like watching a fly clinging to a vertical wall as it edged its way downward—except Erich didn't have any wings to save him if he fell.

Her stomach knotted and sweat coated her palms. The dizzying sensation of height made her queasy.

He should have stayed here. With her. Eventually someone would have come to their rescue.

She shimmied back out of the window slit and paced the floor with knees gone wobbly. Every muffled sound she heard was like an emery board rasping across her nerve endings. She was sure to hear him scream when he fell. The last sound he'd ever make.

There was no need for her to watch.

Oh, Lord, here she was conjuring up the worst case scenario when, in fact, Erich was a skilled climber. She ought to have a little faith in the man. It wasn't as if he was as terrified of heights as she was.

Snatching up one of the journals piled neatly in the corner, she decided her best bet was to think of something else—anything besides the way Erich was only milliseconds from bone-crushing death. Or at the very least, serious injury.

It was one of the journals Erich had told her about—recipes for a moss compress, elderberry wine, pine bark tea, and an unpleasant-sounding concoction that called for the skin of a toad ground up into little pieces.

Her eyes widened.

"That's it!" How could she have forgotten? She'd loved that particular PBS show. Incredibly informative. Odd facts she wouldn't otherwise have learned or even cared about. Now she did.

Ignoring her usual fear of heights, she raced to the window.

"Erich!" she shouted, leaning out as far as she could. "Frederick wasn't a witch! I know what he was up to." Erich didn't respond to her call as he continued to painstakingly descend the tower wall.

Behind her Julianne heard a muttered curse followed by the sound of the door latch sliding open.

Chapter Ten

Erich nearly lost his grip when Julianne called out to him. Admittedly, he wasn't all that far above ground level. But he'd known people to break their ankles falling off something as low as a stepladder. Now was no time to get careless. Particularly since Julianne had evidently found the answers they'd sought.

As he felt for another toe tip pocket, Erna called up to him from the base of the tower, "My goodness, Erich, how clever of you to practice your climbing on our castle wall."

"Oh, no, sister. He is climbing the tower wall to claim our Juli as his bride. It that not romantic? Just like a fairy tale."

Erich stifled an eye-rolling groan, eased the grip of his right hand and found a new purchase for his fingertips. The Sisters had a curious way of leaping to exactly the wrong conclusion.

"Yes, of course." Erna clapped her hands. "Though I think a sprig of edelweiss would have been more than persuasive enough if he wanted to impress Julianne. She is such a sweet girl."

"Climbing is a bit dangerous," Olga agreed.

"Ladies, if you'll back out of the way..." He was only a few feet above the Sisters. If he did, by some chance, slip, he didn't want to fall on them.

"Oh, we won't interfere."

"We both think it quite nice that you and our Juli are getting on so well together. It does seem like quite a long climb, however."

"Ladies! I'm coming *down.*"

"Oh, my, I do hope we have not embarrassed you. We'll just go on back inside, dear, and no one will ever know we caught you doing something so romantic."

"Though why you would want to keep it a secret is beyond me. My Josef used to do romantic things all of the time. It was *so* exciting."

Risking a twisted ankle, Erich dropped the remaining few feet to the ground, managing to avoid a collision with the Sisters.

"Listen to me very carefully, ladies." He tried to cower them with a grim scowl, but they seemed oblivious of his displeasure. Evidently they were immune to fire-breathing dragons, he thought wryly.

From the way the two women were bundled up in hooded jackets, and the envelopes in Erna's hand, he surmised they'd been out to retrieve the day's mail from the box at the end of the long driveway. "Julianne and I were *locked* in the tower room. We couldn't get out, so I climbed *down* the wall."

Like a synchronized pair of long-necked cranes, they raised their heads to look up at the tower.

"Why would you two lock yourselves in the tower?"

A muscle ticked in his jaw. "We didn't. Someone else did."

"It does seem a bit odd," Olga conceded, ignoring Erich's remark. "Perhaps it is some custom Julianne learned in America."

Erna giggled. "Maybe they just wanted to be alone, sister. Have you forgotten what it is like to be young?"

Feeling outnumbered and on the verge of losing control, Erich said, "If you ladies will excuse me, I've got to go let Julianne out of the tower room."

"You'll use the stairs this time, dear? It is really much safer."

"But not nearly as romantic," Olga sighed.

Mentally deciding there was no way to win an argument with the slightly balmy sisters, Erich headed into the castle. In spite of himself, he was fond of the two old women. They were fixtures in the community and had been for a long time. While Erna might not have managed the leaseholdings in quite the same way as Erich would have himself, to his knowledge she had never taken advantage of the tenants. In fact, he suspected she had loaned the farmers money when banks refused. More often than not, it was the Sisters who were there first to offer assistance when a tenant fell ill. They were both good women, though trying, he admitted.

RUSHING DOWN the hallway, Julianne met him at the front door. "Oh, I'm so glad you're all right," she said, barely checking the instinctive need to fly into the safety of Erich's strong arms. Last night she wouldn't have hesitated. Today was a different matter.

He raised his eyebrows in surprise at seeing her. "I'm fine. But how did you get out of the tower room on your own?"

"I don't know. Someone unlocked the door." An invisible someone who had nearly scared Julianne out of her wits. Her heart was still pounding like a drummer showing off, and her knees felt shaky from running down three flights of stairs as if the devil himself was on her heels.

"Who let you out?"

"I was hoping it might have been the Sisters who had somehow—"

"They've been out taking a walk. I met them outside."

"And it wasn't you." Her voice cracked as she drew an uneven breath.

"No, I've just gotten off the wall." As if sensing her near hysteria, Erich gently palmed her cheek. His fingers felt rough and chilly against her overheated face. "Are you all right?"

"Yes . . . no." She swallowed hard. "I thought there was someone in the tower room, Erich. Someone I couldn't see."

Skepticism lowered his brows into a dark line. His eyes were so blue they were like sapphires. "Tell me what happened."

"Well...I was so afraid you might fall that I couldn't stand to watch you doing your Spider-Man imitation, so I picked up one of Frederick's journals to read." The combination of excitement and residual fear drove her words together in a jumble. "I started thumbing through the pages and it turned out it was one of the journals we'd already read. That's when it came to me. What Frederick had been up to all those years ago that made people think he was a witch. Or at least it allowed his enemies to convince an archbishop he was."

"I missed something?"

"It was the business about the toad that gave it away."

"I'm not following you."

"Your great-great-great-grandfather was doing research on folk medicines. Those recipes you found were the ingredients the local people used—probably the midwives, since there weren't many doctors in this remote area in the eighteen hundreds. As Grandma proudly tells anyone who will listen, Lohr am See has always been a bit behind the times."

At the puzzled tilt of his head, she hurried to explain her theory.

"Under every concoction, he wrote down the names of the people who received the medicine. Villagers, would be my guess. Then he made a notation about the patient's recovery. At first I didn't understand what it was all about." She paused only long enough to take a breath. "It's so simple, Erich. He put a plus if the patient got better, a zero if the condition went unchanged, and a minus if the patient got sicker. Or died, I suppose. It was all very logical. He kept meticulous records."

"About the flora and fauna, too. But why toads? They've always been connected with witchcraft and hardly what I'd think of as medicinal. Were the midwives he dealt with practicing witches?"

"No, of course not. They were just passing on information to him that they'd probably learned from their mothers about what cures particular diseases. I saw a PBS television show a couple of years ago. It turns out the skin of some toads has natural antibiotic properties."

"Antibiotic?" His eyes narrowed as he weighed what she had told him. "I still don't understand what toads have to do with you getting out of the tower."

"Nothing. At least not directly. After I hung out the window and shouted at you that I'd found the answer, the door opened. By itself."

"Are you saying Frederick . . ."

"I don't know what I'm saying. But I did hear a man swear. And whoever it was knows we can prove Frederick was falsely accused of witchcraft."

"How can we do that?"

Taking his arm, she tugged him over to the side of the vestibule and lowered her voice. "With the journals and the help of my cousin, Marsha Furst. She's Olga's granddaughter and she works at the PBS station in Los Angeles. We don't see each other very often, but I always kind of watch for her shows."

"Her shows on toads? You're going too fast for me, Julianne. How is your cousin going to help?"

"Don't you see? She can get us a videotape of the program I saw about toads." Her fears forgotten for the moment, Julianne smiled at him smugly. She'd solved the mystery, by damn! "A judge will have to believe it then. Frederick was a scientist, not a witch."

He looked at her incredulously. Slowly, as realization dawned, his lips curved into the most devastating smile she'd ever seen. His cheeks creased. At the corners of his eyes, crinkles appeared.

"Frederick never should have been hung." Emotion choked his voice until it was husky and so damn sexy Julianne wanted to bottle it.

"No. They used the good he was trying to do and turned it against him."

"The castle never should have been confiscated."

"Never." Caught up in the excitement of discovery, she grinned at him. "It's the most unfair thing I've ever heard of."

In an exuberant move, he spanned her waist with his hands and lifted her off her feet as if she were buoyant. She had to steady herself by resting her hands on his shoulders.

"It all makes a bizarre kind of sense."

"Of course it does. I got an 'A' in Logic 101."

His laugh was deep and wonderful, as though a heavy burden had been lifted from his chest. "At long last the Langlois can take their rightful place in Lohr am See."

"There certainly won't be any reason for the villagers to accuse you of witchcraft." A little magical seduction, possibly, but what woman would complain?

"More than that, Julianna. Far more than that. We can now fulfill our destiny."

He lowered her until their lips were level. The kiss he claimed was a sweet moment of triumph, hot and hungry and filled with promise—

Julianne went rigid. *What destiny?* she wondered. And what of her grandmother?

"Erich..." she protested against his lips. "You promised Erna wouldn't lose her home."

"She won't. You still have my word." He lowered Julianne to the floor. "Back to the tower room, my brilliantly logical and beautiful friend. We've got to get that journal safely in our hands before Frederick, or his impostor, makes off with it."

A cold wave of air swept into the hallway as the front door opened.

"There you are, children," Erna called, beaming as she wiped her muddy feet on the Welcome mat.

"We do hope you are suitably impressed, Juli," Olga said, following her sister into the entryway. "Erich is so forceful. So much like my Josef was. Austrian men are like that, you know. Imagine, planning to climb all that way—"

"Excuse us, ladies." Erich grabbed Julianne's hand. "There's something we need to do."

He pulled Julianne down the hallway, but before they had gone far she heard Olga say, "Young men are so impulsive these days. Impatient, too. I do believe Josef had far better control."

"What's she talking about?" Julianne asked.

"I'll explain later," he muttered.

They turned the corner of the long corridor and were about to go up the stairs to the tower when the door behind them to the cellar snapped shut.

Erich swore. "We missed him!"

"Missed who? Will you please tell me what's going on?" she pleaded.

He whipped open the door. "The ghost of Schloss Lohr just went down those steps." He flicked on the light.

To Julianne's dismay, what she saw was not a ghost but one of Frederick's leather-bound journals *floating* downward above the stairway. Nobody was there. Just the journal. In midair. Moving slowly.

Goose bumps raced down her spine and her mouth went dry. "Er-ich . . ."

"I know." He shielded her with his body. "Whoever you are, I think it's time we had a little talk."

The journal stopped its flight down the stairs. Next to it, *holding* the book, a man materialized from what had been nothing more than dust motes.

"It's him," Julianne gasped. Her nagging ghost, knobby knees, lederhosen and bushy mustache included. "Frederick."

"*Verdammt!* You have been nothing but a nuisance since you arrived, *Fräulein*. And now you and this young pup are going to ruin everything!" His face turning an apoplectic shade of red, he shook a fist at them. "I want you out of my castle now. Both of you. This very minute!"

"Easy, fellow. We aren't here to hurt you." Edging down the stairs, Erich wanted to calm the old man. Warm-blooded or apparition, he could see the Langlois family resemblance—long nose, strong jaw, and telltale blue eyes. Amazing. But a ghost? It would take Erich a while to adjust to that possibility.

"You want this journal, do you not?" He backed toward the wine racks at the shadowed rear of the cellar. "If I had had good sense, I would have destroyed my journals years ago."

"Why? What harm can they do?"

"Fool! I would have hoped my descendants had passed on a smidgen of common sense to my heirs. Apparently no such good fortune made it as far as your generation."

Erich bristled at the insult.

Julianne found her voice. "Are you the ghost of Frederick Langlois?"

"Who did you think I was? The plumber?" He pulled his shirt collar away from his neck. An ugly welt the width of a hangman's noose circled his throat.

"If you are indeed my ancestor—"

"To my great displeasure, I assure you."

"Then surely you'd want to help me clear your name. You weren't a witch, were you?"

"Whether or not I was a witch matters little now. They damn well hung me."

"That must have hurt a great deal," Julianne said sympathetically. "And I can imagine how frightened you must have been as you walked up the gallows steps."

He lifted his chin. "I went to my death bravely, without a hood so I could see my accusers till the end. As well a Langlois should."

"Erich is very brave, too. Just the other day he climbed a very dangerous mountain to rescue a man who'd fallen. A young villager. Now that I've had a chance to talk with you, I can see Erich inherited his courage from you. As well as his good looks."

In spite of his continuing antagonistic gaze, Frederick stood a little straighter. His chest puffed out.

Erich smiled to himself. He could see the old guy, ghost or not, succumbing to Julianne's charm. She had an uncanny knack for making people feel good about themselves. A time or two he'd fallen under the same spell and now regretted he had distrusted her. Old habits died hard, he realized.

"Are you aware," Erich asked, "that after you died, your wife and child suffered terribly?"

"It was Berker's fault. That lying scoundrel Egon had always been jealous of my landholdings, though he

had never been willing to do a lick of work on his own."
A sheen of tears appeared in his eyes. "I tried to come
to the aid of my beloved Kathe and my son. But it was
decades before I could maneuver properly in this out-of-
body state I found myself in. Damn inconvenient at
first."

His scowl melted into a wicked grin directed at Julianne. "Did manage to drive Cousin Egon stark raving
mad, however, by haunting my castle. He found little
joy in his illicit ownership of Schloss Lohr."

"In retaliation, he and the villagers made life a living hell for all of your descendants," Erich told him.
"Like your Kathe, my sister and I continue to suffer
ostracism in the village."

"So where is your spine, young pup? I have no wish
to claim any weak-kneed kin as mine. Fight back! That
is my motto."

"That's exactly why Erich needs the journal. He's
going to prove you weren't a witch and never should
have been hung."

"Have you so much as bothered to consider the consequences of such an action?" the ghost bellowed. In a
fury, he paced across the cellar, then turned to glare at
them. "Well? Have you?"

"Erich and his sister—"

"Not the consequences for *them*, you little instiga-
tor! For me! *And* your sweet grandmother, I might
add."

"Grandma?" Julianne felt herself pale. "What do
you mean?"

"If you and this young pup of yours make everything neat and tidy about my death, and even—God forbid—get the archbishop to consecrate my remains—I will have to cross over to the other side."

"Why wouldn't you want that to happen?" Erich asked cautiously.

"Because, my dear, simple-minded heir, this is *my* castle. I have been caretaker here for nearly two hundred years. Under no circumstances do I intend to abandoned Schloss Lohr to the incompetent hands of those who have no respect for the past and would allow this magnificent building to collapse in ruin."

"Magnificent?" Erich questioned. "There are those in the village who think it is no more than an ugly pile of stone."

"There! He has no instinct for quality or style. You see what I mean?"

"You mean, you're afraid to die," Julianne ventured in a softly spoken guess.

His eyes blazed at her. "Nonsense. Ask yourself this, young lady. If I were to *die,* as you so neatly put it, who would look after your grandmother and her deaf-as-stone niece? What do you suppose would happen to them if left to their own devices?"

"They're getting up in years, but they seem—"

"*Twice* during the winter months they forgot to close the screen across the fireplace. Sparks, my dear, have a way of landing on flammable objects. In spite of stone walls, my castle is not fireproof. Certainly not the contents, including the two charming women who are currently in residence."

"Everybody forgets occasionally—"

"The bathtub overflowed only weeks ago. Ants regularly attack rubbish Olga neglects to remove from the kitchen. Bills are not paid in a timely fashion unless I put them directly under Erna's nose. *And* find her glasses for her. Need I elaborate further?"

"None of that matters," Erich insisted, striding toward Frederick. "If the Sisters need a caretaker, we'll make arrangements. The Langlois name needs to be cleared, and will be, no matter what you say." He reached for the journal.

"No, Erich. Wait!"

He turned toward her, and in that instant Frederick bolted toward the stairs, the journal tucked under his arm. He was surprisingly agile, though perhaps a ghost wasn't constrained by age and gravity the way humans were.

Erich started to follow. In a moment of panic, Julianne blocked his path, restraining him with her hands pressed against his chest.

"I can't let you send my grandmother to an old folks' home. She'd be miserable. She'd die, Erich. So would Olga."

The door to the main floor of the castle slammed shut behind the vanishing ghost of Frederick.

"We're not talking about—" Erich tried to slip past her, but Julianne wouldn't let him go.

"Will you please slow down and think about what's at stake here. Please, Erich. For my sake."

A muscle ticked in his jaw. "What about Helene? If I don't clear the Langlois name—"

"Then she won't be able to marry some guy you don't very much like anyway and who shouldn't give a damn about what happened more than a hundred years ago. Would that be so awful? Would it be worth the price of my grandmother's happiness in her few remaining years?"

She could almost see his mind working, weighing the importance of one life against the other, the futures of two women Julianne believed he cared about. She sensed he was a fair man. A courageous man. But she didn't know what sort of a decision he would make where his sister's happiness was involved. Both he and Helene had suffered a great deal at the hands of the villagers. She could hardly blame either of them for hoping the future would be better.

She lowered her hands. "It's your choice, Erich."

The weight of his conscience pressed down on his shoulders as Erich placed his foot on the first stair leading to the main floor of the castle. By all rights, the *Langlois* castle, he reminded himself.

"Frederick is probably gone by now, so I have no choice. For the moment."

Slowly he climbed the stairs. He'd come so damn close to his goal, now . . .

Julianne was right. How could he jeopardize the lives of two dotty old women for the sake of his sister's happiness? She had her whole life before her.

But a ghost as the Sisters' caretaker? No one would ever believe that.

He looked back down the stairs at Julianne. The glare from the unshielded light bulb combined with her silver blond hair to create a halo effect. Maybe ghosts and angels both resided in Schloss Lohr, he mused in a rare fanciful moment.

"Will you at least contact your cousin about the tape?" he asked. "Then later, perhaps..." He let the thought drift away. "I'll have to talk with my sister."

She met his gaze steadily, concern and questions evident in her hazel eyes. "The Sisters were hoping you'd stay for dinner."

"I'm not sure that is a good idea."

"Why not? Because even after Frederick has made his wishes quite clear—and the consequences—you're still determined to reveal the truth about him?"

"I will weigh my decision carefully, Julianne. That is all I can promise for now."

Chapter Eleven

A china cup sailed past Erich's head and crashed against the kitchen wall behind him. He grimaced. All decisions had consequences, including the one he'd made on the short drive from Schloss Lohr to his home.

"That's enough, Helene!"

"You are not being fair!" she wailed.

"You're acting like a spoiled two-year-old."

"And you are acting like that American has you wrapped around her little finger," she countered. "Why do you listen to her? I am your sister and you are going to ruin my entire life, all because of that woman."

"No, Helene, that's not true." He couldn't remember a time when he'd been so angry with his sister. For years he'd blamed the villagers for the way she acted, often petulant and self-centered. Now he wondered if he was the one at fault for having indulged her too much. It was time she took some responsibility for her own happiness. In fact, he doubted she was mature enough to marry at all.

With effort, he forced himself to remain calm. "I suggest you tell Paul that Frederick Langlois wasn't a witch—"

"Because a *ghost* told you so? He would laugh in my face."

"And that if he loves you, whatever happened a century ago is of no importance now."

"He will think I'm crazy if I give him some story about toads. No one in the village will believe—"

"The story is true. Not even that should be important to him if you both love each other."

"You do not understand! He is about to be promoted at the bank. He has his reputation to think of. He can't risk his credibility with the investors with some wild story about *toads.*"

"Investors in what? The bank is sound, isn't it? Who he is married to won't affect that."

"He does not plan to work for the bank forever, Erich. He has ambitions. He has plans for our future." A hiccuppy sob caught in her throat and her face got all splotchy red with the threat of tears. "He says we'll be rich. I will have a new car every year. And not have to live in a hovel like this." Her lips curled disdainfully as she looked around the outdated kitchen. "I am sick of this place."

Erich admitted their modest cottage left a great deal to be desired, but it was as much as he had ever needed for his comfort. He could understand through a woman's eyes the verdict would be different. Idly he wondered what Julianne would think of his home, and immediately shrugged off the thought. She was no doubt used to far more elegance than he could provide.

She deserved a castle.

His decision to not pursue clearing the Langlois name meant Schloss Lohr would someday belong to Julianne. It seemed right and proper suddenly that that should be the case. In spite of what Frederick had thought, Erich, too, appreciated the ancient history of the castle. Perhaps when the Sisters were gone Julianne would allow him to oversee the castle and its lands— jointly with his irascible ghostly ancestor, of course.

"If you'd like, I'll talk to Paul for you," he said. Perhaps Erich could also suggest they wait a few years before they married, time enough to let Helene grow up.

"No. I will tell him myself!" She ran to the back door, yanked it open and was gone before Erich could stop her.

He swore under his breath. Kneeling, he scooped up the shards of broken china. It was not only Helene who had suffered as a Langlois. Their mother had endured so much harassment she had fled rather than face the villagers. Her actions had certainly taught Erich well. Unlike his father, he would never ask a woman to bear the burden of accepting his name. Not as matters stood now. Nor would the situation change in the foreseeable future.

Decisions had consequences. All of them.

Heading for his workroom to prepare his equipment for the next climb, Erich knew what he had to do. What surprised him was how much this new decision hurt.

THE SISTERS had already gone to bed when Julianne heard the knock on the door. She'd been sitting in the cozy parlor room. Waiting. And hoping. Though since Erich had not appeared for dinner, she had no reason to expect his return.

But her hearing had been so attuned to the normal sounds in the castle, she would have heard a mouse sneeze. His soft tap on the door was like a welcome clap of thunder to her ears.

"I wasn't sure you'd still be awake," he said when she opened the door.

"I was waiting for you." With a wary smile he acknowledged her honesty. She really ought to learn to be more coy, she thought. With Erich, she doubted she'd ever learn the knack, and cursed herself for being so foolish. "Come in."

Once inside the entryway, Erich hesitated. The silence between them crackled with the same intensity as electricity raised the hair on a person's arms an instant before lightning split the sky. Unanswered questions rode on every supercharged atom. Had he given up his quest for the journals? Did he remember how they had made love last night? Or how this morning their fragile trust had been shaken?

He swallowed visibly, as though he had difficulty in finding the words he wanted. Or perhaps the words he intended to say had stuck in his throat. "I came to tell you goodbye."

A knife thrust into her heart would have been less painful. "Goodbye?"

"I have to go to Salzburg in the morning to pick up a party of climbers."

"Didn't all this come up rather suddenly? I mean, you hadn't mentioned—"

"I've been distracted lately, Julianne. I've been scheduled to lead this climbing party for some time." His voice was cool, almost impersonal. "It's how I make my living."

"Yes, of course. How long—"

"A week. They wanted to try a couple of different peaks."

"Oh." There was little time remaining in her vacation and most of that time he'd be gone. The sharp pain in her heart eased into a hollow ache she knew would remain there for the entire seven days.

"I've talked with Helene. I told her there is proof Frederick wasn't a witch, but that we wouldn't be making use of that information. Other issues are more important."

A relieved sigh escaped Julianne. "How did she take the news?"

"She's furious, but she'll recover. I thought while I am in Salzburg I'd investigate an art school there. She has shown some talent in drawing."

"Moving there might be best for her. Particularly if Paul is cruel enough to refuse to marry her."

"Yes, that's what I thought."

Julianne recognized that his terse dragon persona had slipped back into place and the man who had lovingly taught her about passion had vanished into his dark cave. "What's wrong, Erich? You seem—"

"It would be best if tonight was a permanent goodbye, Julianne. You will be returning to America soon and I no longer have a reason to visit Schloss Lohr to search out the truth about Frederick." He lifted his broad shoulders in a fatalistic shrug. "Delaying the inevitable seems pointless."

Pointless. An apt epitaph for a vacation fling.

She put on her brave face, the one carefully designed to hide hurt and tears. "Hey, then, it's been great. Have a good climb with your friends."

"I will. Assuming the weather clears." His slow perusal brought heat to her face, but she didn't flinch. "I trust you will enjoy the rest of your stay in Austria."

"Sure." She felt like she'd swallowed a pack of razor blades and they'd all come apart in her throat. "I'll probably take in the local pub another time or two. And Erna said there's an interesting salt mine that's open to tourists not far from here. That ought to be fun." Root canals were great sport, too, she'd been told.

She stepped around him to open the door. "Look me up if you ever get to the States."

"Yes, I'll do that."

At his softly spoken lie, something shattered inside Julianne. By sheer force of will, she held herself together until he was gone and the door shut behind him.

THE KRAMPAS character danced around the village square bringing smiles from lingering market day shoppers with his noontime antics. But Julianne didn't respond.

It still stung that the village museum keeper had accused her of being a traitor to the Berker family. Worse, Julianne's heart hadn't stopped aching since Erich had told her goodbye. Finding a smile at all was a painfully difficult exercise in self-control. It was easier to save the effort for when she was with the Sisters. She didn't want them to realize anything was wrong.

Nearly seven full days, each of them agonizingly long, had slipped by. She would have thought by now her natural resiliency would have kicked in. It always had before when her heart had taken a blow.

Not this time.

Two days ago she had delivered the videotape her cousin had sent from Los Angeles. Since Erich had made it abundantly clear he didn't want to see her again, it seemed wiser to simply leave the tape with his sister while he was away. The reception she had received from Helene was understandably less than cordial.

"Erich is not here," Helene had said abruptly when she'd opened the back door to their small cottage. Her dark hair was mussed and her eyes red-rimmed as though she'd been crying.

"I know. He asked me to get this for him." Julianne had extended the videotape to Erich's sister. "I'm not sure he still wants it. The tape would help clear Frederick's name, but now..."

Helene had snatched the container from her hand. "But now you have ruined everything and the Langlois will always be outcasts in the village. I wish you had never come to Austria."

"Look, I'm sorry about your boyfriend. I'm sure, in time, you'll get over—"

"Never!"

With a juvenile flair for the dramatic, Helene had slammed the door in Julianne's face.

Sighing at the memory, Julianne glanced up at the peaks that surrounded Lohr am See. Until today the weatherman had provided beautiful weather for Erich's climb. Now an overcast sky threatened rain and Julianne found herself worrying about his safety.

"Fool!" she muttered. "You'd worry a worm right out of his hole, given half a chance."

An elderly woman examining a display of apricots imported from Spain gave Julianne a curious look, then moved away to consider the next vendor's wares.

Julianne had explored all of the village streets, and most of the nearby walking trails, but she set off toward the south. She'd told the Sisters not to wait lunch for her. She had little appetite, and it seemed a shame to waste Olga's culinary skills on her. She'd do better at dinner if she had some exercise. Not that the persistent lump in her throat allowed much room to swallow even the tastiest meal.

As the early summer had progressed, new wildflowers had appeared in the meadows. She concentrated on identifying those she passed and hoped the fresh, clear air would renew her spirit, much as each new season revitalized the soil.

Soon she was well out of the village and lost in the solitude of the landscape.

The attack came from behind her. An arm around her neck. Choking her.

Julianne screamed and struggled. A mugger, she thought, more than willing to hand over the few Austrian schillings she had in her pocket rather than forfeit her life. If only he'd give her the chance.

She twisted and turned as a black hood descended over her head. The instant before all went to darkness, Julianne caught a glimpse of the grotesque wooden mask of the Krampas glaring at her, the horns and red painted lips all the more frightening for being so unexpected.

"Hans, you can't do this," she protested.

He yanked her arms behind her back and whipped a rope around her wrists. Caught off guard, she hardly had a chance to struggle, much less escape.

"Please, Hans. Don't do this." Terror clawed at her. She'd never had to deal with a madman before. "Grandma Erna isn't going to lose the castle. I promise. Nothing's going to change."

Wordlessly, he shoved her forward.

She stumbled. With a ruthless jerk, he steadied her, then pushed her forward again.

This is crazy, she thought. If she was going to get mugged, it should have been in downtown Minneapolis, or in some other big city, not in a tiny rural village in the Alps.

She let out another scream.

Her reward was a sharp cuff across her head that brought tears to her eyes.

"Damn it! I've never done anything—"

With a grunt, he shoved her up against something hard. A car, she thought, just before she was pushed inside and made to lie on the floor of the back seat. It smelled of wet fibers and moldering dirt. Her stomach roiled with nauseating fear as she sensed a cover being pulled over her prone body. She was going to die at the hands of a maniac and there seemed little she could do to stop him.

Moments later the car started.

A bumpy ride led to a new ordeal of marching up a hillside, over a rocky, ankle-twisting path. Time and again, Julianne tried to convince Hans he was making a mistake. But her words were met only with silence. She knew they were gaining altitude because her breathing was becoming more labored with each step. Her kidnapper was struggling, too, and his breath rasped more loudly than hers.

Good grief, she thought, giddy with fear, the old man may have a heart attack before all this is over.

A fine mist began to dampen her arms and her footing became even less secure. Her feet slipped on the wet ground. She shivered, sure she was about to plummet off the edge into some deep ravine. In some vague way she was glad she couldn't see how narrow the trail was they were following, or how far she might fall.

Why didn't he simply kill her instead of putting her through this ordeal? she wondered even as she recognized the answer lay in the sickness of his mind.

He yanked her to an abrupt stop. Her legs were trembling and her breath came in frightened little gulps.

The icy cold of metal sliding across flesh eased between her wrists. The rope binding her wrists parted and blood sped with tingling fury to her fingertips. With a quick tug, the hood was pulled from her head. But before she had a chance to react, her kidnapper shoved her into a low, squat building made of stone and she tumbled to the ground. Her palms stung as pebbles dug into her hands.

Hinges creaked. Wood thudded against wood. Scrambling to her feet, she raced to the door.

"Wait! Don't leave me here!" she shouted. She pushed with all her might against the unyielding door and heard a bolt fall into place. She rammed her shoulder against the thick planks, but knew it was useless.

Changing tactics, she tried to see out the high, narrow window. "Hans! Please..." she cried to his departing figure. He walked purposefully through the circle of miniature monoliths where witches were said to have once danced.

"Help me!" she screamed. "Somebody please help me!"

There was no reply. Only the distant echo of her voice drifting away.

Fear swelled in Julianne's throat. She whirled to examine her cell, which felt like a prison. The two windows were far too narrow to provide a means of escape; the door too solid for even a battering ram to have any effect.

She started at a faint scurrying sound across the room. She could barely make out the outline of the resident toad staring back at her in unblinking curiosity. His tongue darted out to test the air.

"Oh, God . . ." she groaned, backing away.

Slowly, she sank to the ground in the corner opposite the toad. An unholy dampness crept into her bones, chilling her.

Dear God, where was Erich? And would he ever learn what had become of her? And what of the Sisters?

Outside, a rising wind blew a keening sound that brought to mind the eerie image of witches dancing on a moonless night.

Chapter Twelve

Erich ripped open the envelope he'd found on the kitchen table.

He had expected to be back to Lohr am See earlier in the day, but his climbing party had insisted on a late departure from base camp that morning. Then highway construction—a plague during the summer months—had further delayed his return from Salzburg by several hours. He was tired and dirty and eager for a hot shower, as well as a good night's sleep. He'd always found solace in the mountains. This trip had been a disappointing exception. His thoughts had been of Julianne—the silken smoothness of her skin, the easy way she smiled, the warmth of her lips, and how he would never taste them again—not on the view from the peaks he was climbing.

For a moment he stared without comprehension at the scrambled message on the plain white stationery. Then the meaning of the words snipped from newspapers began to register with frightening clarity.

Julianne kidnapped. Frederick Langlois' journal the price of the ransom. Or she wouldn't live to see another sunrise.

Erich's weary legs weakened and he sat heavily on a kitchen chair. *Dear God in Heaven,* he prayed, though he knew there was no Lord above who would recognize his unfamiliar voice.

A painful knot formed in his gut. He couldn't let anything happen to Julianne. She was far too important to him, too precious to die at the hands of a kidnapper.

He crumpled the ransom note in his fist. The instructions were clear. Before the evening mass he was to take the journal that would clear Frederick's name to the church in Lohr am See and secrete it under the kneeling bench at the altar. The kidnapper would retrieve the journal and only when he knew he was safe from pursuit would he inform Erich of Julianne's whereabouts.

To save Julianne, Erich would gladly have done what the kidnapper asked. Hell, he would have given a king's ransom to save her. Even his own life, if necessary.

The realization of how much he had come to care for Julianne wrenched through Erich like he'd been yanked up hard from a fall at the end of a long rope.

But Erich didn't have the damn journal.

Frederick did!

His mind searched through a very short list of options. There was no way he could involve the police in a kidnapping that involved pleading with a ghost for his help. The authorities would be sure he'd lost his mind.

With time already running out, there would be no margin for explanations.

Leaving his climbing gear in a heap on the kitchen floor, he searched the house. There was no sign of Helene, and his stomach knotted on the bitter bile of guilt that she might be behind Julianne's kidnapping. His sister had been so angry that the Langlois name would not be cleared, she might well have been tempted to do something desperate.

Adrenaline surging, Erich raced for the back door. He had to convince Frederick to give up the journal, at least long enough for him to discover where the kidnapper had taken Julianne. Assuming Frederick hadn't already burned the damn thing!

He reached Schloss Lohr with his heart pounding so hard an onlooker would have guessed that he was terribly out of shape and that he'd run, not driven, the few kilometers between the cottage and the castle.

He hammered on the door with his fist.

Erna responded to his urgent knocking. "Ah, what a surprise, dear boy. How nice of you to drop by."

"Is Julianne here?" he asked with little hope he'd get the answer he so desperately wanted.

"Why, no. And we are getting concerned. She is not usually this late returning from her little walks and it is almost suppertime. But then, she has been a bit preoccupied of late. I do hope you two young people—"

"Where's Frederick?"

"Frederick?" Her eyes, magnified behind thick lenses, blinked rapidly.

"I need to see Frederick. Now! It's a matter of life and death." Julianne's life, the most precious life he could think of. "Your granddaughter has been kidnapped."

"Oh, my..." Erna's hand flew to her chest.

Frantically, he looked around the entry as though there might be an ancestral apparition lurking nearby. Where the hell would a ghost hang out when he wasn't doing ghostly things?

The tower room!

That first night Erich had slipped into the castle and successfully made his way to the library, he'd seen a shadow in the tower window as he'd left. And later, that's where Frederick had taken the journals. To the place where he felt most at home.

Erich burst past Erna at a run.

He took the three flights of stairs two at a time. Exploding into the tower room, he shouted, "Frederick! Where the hell are you?"

The old guy materialized, his hair rumpled, eyelids drooping, as though he'd been rudely awaken from a nap. He scowled at Erich. "What do you want, young pup?"

"It's Julianne. She's been kidnapped."

If a ghost could go gray, Frederick did just that, as though every drop of nonexistent blood had drained from his face. "What do you mean?"

Erich told him about the ransom note as succinctly as possible, then asked, "Do you still have the journal?"

The old man's gaze shot across the room in guilty admission toward the heap of journals that had not yet been moved back to the library. "And if I do?"

"I'm going to do what the kidnapper wants. I'm taking the journal to the church. And you're going with me."

"I do not go outside the castle. Indeed, I have not done so in more than a century. The Sisters, as well as their predecessors at Schloss Lohr, have been such inveterate gossips that I have had no need to leave these hallowed walls to learn what is going on in the village."

"But you could leave if you wanted to."

Frederick "humphed" and cleared his throat. "I suppose it is possible. It simply has not seemed necessary. This is my home, you know, and it requires a great deal of my attention."

"If whoever is after the journal gets it, you'll lose your home and pass over to the next life, Frederick. And if he—or she—doesn't get what he wants, Julianne's life will be on your conscience. You've got to help me."

Amazingly, Frederick straightened, the appeal to his more noble instincts instilling a strength to his spine that must surely have reflected the village leader he had been more than a century ago. "I take it you have a plan."

"I do," Erich agreed. "Listen carefully..."

ERICH SLIPPED into the church as inconspicuously as possible. Frederick was with him, but had remained invisible in case the kidnapper was watching. Or anyone else, for that matter.

The candles burning on the altar cast a quavering light around the shadowed chapel. Except for two parishioners whose heads were covered by dark scarves, the sanctuary was empty. Only the muted sound of rosary beads clicking in rhythm could be heard.

Erich slipped the journal under the kneeling bench, per instructions. The kidnapper had been clever to select a holy day for his scheme. Dozens of people would pass through the church this evening, most of them kneeling in this very spot for the priest's blessing. The penitent who removed the journal would go entirely unnoticed.

Except by Frederick.

"Are you all set?" Erich asked under his breath.

"Do not trouble yourself. I will follow the culprit," Frederick replied with a disembodied voice. "The journal will be back safely in my hands before he knows what has happened."

"But not before I learn where he has taken Julianne."

"I understand."

Erich left the church the way he had come.

Then he took up his vigil beside the phone in his house.

The minutes dragged by with agonizing slowness. He paced the length of the kitchen and parlor and back again, never allowing himself to be more than a few steps from the phone. Sweat beaded his forehead and fear knotted in his gut. What if his plan went awry? Relying on a ghost as a partner might well prove to be a folly, just this side of madness.

Outside, the weather was deteriorating rapidly. Even in summer the temperature at higher elevations could drop suddenly to a bitter cold.

Where had the kidnapper taken Julianne? Or had he already killed her? Erich dreaded the answers to his questions. Through no fault of her own, Julianne was paying a high price for her association with a Langlois. Just as his mother had been made to pay dearly.

In the distance, the church bell marked the end of mass.

The phone rang.

Erich's hand trembled as he snatched the instrument from the wall. "Where is she?" he barked into the phone.

A muffled voice, well disguised, spoke. "Where the witches dance." Then the caller severed the connection.

He stared mutely at the phone for several heartbeats before the implication of the words settled in. He'd have to hurry, he realized. If Julianne wasn't dressed properly for this weather, she'd be frozen before he reached her.

FREDERICK FOLDED his arms across his chest, quite pleased with his success at following the man who had retrieved the journal from the church. With the phone call completed to Erich, it was time the kidnapper paid a price for abducting such a charming young lady as Julianne.

Ah, yes, had he been younger—*much* younger, he conceded—Frederick would have set his cap for her himself. And provided his woefully inadequate heir a good deal of competition, he surmised without an ounce of braggadocio. Indeed, in his day, he had cut a fine figure of a man as far as the fairer sex was concerned.

"I believe you have something that belongs to me," he said, adding vibrato to his disembodied voice for a ghostly touch.

The villain whirled. "Who is it?"

"The author of the book you hold."

The pathetically confused kidnapper spun around again. "Where are you? Come out where I can see you."

Picking up a pillow from the couch, Frederick sailed it across the room. "I am everywhere, for I am your worthless conscience."

"No, I do not believe—" He backed away from the spot where the pillow had landed.

Frederick flicked the light switch several times. "Do you believe this?"

In a panic, he picked up a vase from the table and threw it in Frederick's direction. "Show yourself!"

Ducking easily, Frederick circled behind the villain and tweaked his ear.

"Ouch!" He spun around, only to have his nose twisted sharply in the process. "What are you doing? Who are you?"

Frederick laughed, a fiendish sound. He couldn't remember the last time he'd had such fun. In spite of his obligations at Schloss Lohr, he really ought to get out and about more often.

SHE'D NEVER been so cold. Or afraid.

Julianne's teeth chattered uncontrollably. Her cotton blouse offered little protection against the chill air and she hugged herself for what small warmth her icy hands had to offer.

She'd lost track of the time hours ago. In the darkness, she couldn't see her watch. The only thing marking the time was the wailing song of the wind. Or maybe it was the echoing cry of witches being burned at the stake centuries ago.

Julianne didn't know. And somehow, with each passing minute, it mattered less and less as a cold numbness settled into her limbs.

Something thumped against the shelter door.

She swallowed a scream. Hans had come back for her, she thought wildly, and she didn't want to die at the hands of a madman.

Though nearly frozen, she forced her fingers to close around a fist-size rock she'd found to use as a weapon. She wouldn't go easily, she promised herself. And maybe, with luck, she could lure the old man into believing she was already dead, or dying, and catch him off guard.

A blast of cold air blew into the shelter as the door swung open. Through slitted eyes, Julianne watched a column of light flit across the dirt floor. She held her breath. Giving him a chance to get close was her only possibility of escape. Yet she shuddered at the thought. If he touched her...

Cold, gloved fingers stroked her cheek.

She screamed. With all her might, she swung her fist at him, gratified by the way the rock connected with something solid.

"Damn!" he grunted. "Julianna, it's me. Erich." He grabbed her wrist, restraining her before she could land a second blow.

"Oh, Erich..." she sobbed, dropping the rock as she threw herself into his welcoming embrace.

He held her tight, and she trembled against him like a leaf quivering in a windstorm, each shiver telegraphing how close she was to hypothermia.

"It's all right, Julianna," he whispered. Relief surged through him that he had arrived in time. Barely. "We have to get you warmed up."

He eased her grip from around his neck, then shrugged out of his backpack and removed his down-filled jacket. "Who did this to you?" he asked as he helped her put on his coat. Her arms were icy cold; her teeth chattered like Spanish castanets. He imagined at that moment if he could get his hands on the person who had put Julianne's life at risk, he would have strangled him. *Or her.*

"Hans." She gulped a shivery breath. "He attacked me without any reason—"

Surprise stilled his hands. "You mean, the museum curator?" Erich wouldn't have believed the old man capable of any crime except a few meaningless threats. But he had acted strangely in the village square the other day. He supposed anything was possible.

"He was wearing that horrible mask."

"The Krampas costume." He pulled off his gloves.

She nodded. "I was so frightened, Erich. He's a lunatic. I thought he was going to kill me."

Taking her hands in his, Erich rubbed vigorously to restore warmth to her chilled fingers. Her hands were so delicate compared to his. And soft. In spite of his best intentions, he remembered how her hands had felt caressing his bare flesh that night they had made love.

Even as his groin tightened, he forcefully shoved the wayward thought aside. "Did you actually see Hans? Or just the mask?"

"I—I'm sure it was him. Who else could it have been?"

Erich was afraid to speculate, afraid the answer would lead to his sister and her boyfriend. They'd find out soon enough when they returned to learn what Frederick had discovered about the kidnapper.

She shuddered again against the cold.

Turning, Erich untied the bedroll he'd lashed to his backpack and spread it out on the ground.

"What are you doing?" she asked.

"You need to get in the sleeping bag to get warm. I'll make you some tea."

"I'll be all right," she insisted, struggling to stand up. "I just want to go home. Back to Schloss Lohr."

"It has begun to snow and the trail is too slippery to travel safely in the dark. We'll wait till morning."

"But you made it here all right."

His lips twitched into a suggestion of a smile. "Haven't you guessed? I'm part mountain goat."

"But what if Hans comes back for me?" she asked tremulously.

Barely controlling a renewed burst of rage, his fist clenched tightly around the small one-burner stove he pulled from his pack. "I would think that would be a very dangerous decision for Hans to make."

Despite her continued objections, Julianne crawled into the sleeping bag. Her shivers had slowed and she seemed to be breathing more easily. Erich left the shelter momentarily to fill a cup with snow, then returned to melt it over the flame. He was acutely aware of Julianne's questioning gaze following his every movement.

Never in a lifetime of self-control had he found his response to a woman so unruly. A week ago he'd vowed never to see her again. Now he was consumed by thoughts of how she had looked gilded by firelight, naked and yielding in his arms. And how afraid he'd been for her safety when he had read the ransom note.

"Did I hurt you when I hit you with the rock?" she asked softly.

His hand went to his temple where he felt a scab of dried blood. "No, you didn't hurt me." But he ached now in a far more painful way than any blow he'd received to the head.

She wet her lips and that small movement sent a bolt of heat to his loins. "How did you know where to find me?"

"When your kidnapper got the ransom he had demanded—"

"Ransom?"

"The journal we discovered that proved Frederick wasn't a witch."

"Why on earth would Hans want that?"

"If it *was* Hans who kidnapped you, he probably thought he was protecting your grandmother."

"You sound like you think it was someone else."

He dipped the tea bag into the steaming water. "Possibly."

"But who?"

Meeting her gaze levelly, he said, "Helene feels she has a great deal to lose if the Langlois name is not cleared."

For an instant her eyes fluttered closed and a sigh escaped her lips. "I'm sorry."

"I hope I'm wrong."

"So do I, Erich. So do I." Distress and sympathy weighted her words.

Along with the tea, he offered her trail mix and strips of dried beef. She ate sparingly.

He marveled that Julianne, who had come so close to losing her life, would be concerned about the individual who might well have put her in harm's way. He suspected there was enormous strength in a woman who could think of someone else before herself. Compassion demanded a great deal from a person. Yet Julianne gave hers without a second thought.

Her simple acts of generosity made him feel things he hadn't believed he was capable of feeling. In a way, that frightened him more than teetering on a ledge hundreds of meters above the ground without even a safety rope.

He shivered and held his palms toward the cooking flame. The wind outside was still blowing down the canyons and the temperature continued to drop.

"You're cold without your jacket," she said.

"I'll be fine. It's time you got some sleep."

She pulled back one corner of the bedroll. "We can share."

A lump formed in his throat. Other parts of his anatomy tightened, as well. "I don't think that's a good idea, Julianne." His voice was more husky with need than he cared to admit.

"I won't bite, Erich. But I'm not going to let you freeze, either." She moved over to allow him as much space as possible.

To not accept her invitation would be foolish. It was damn cold and he was, after all, a grown man fully capable of controlling his baser instincts.

Except around Julianne, he thought with a defeated groan.

He switched off the flashlight. Under cover of darkness, he gritted his teeth against the coming ordeal and crawled into the bedroll with her. Instantly, she spooned herself against his back and he discovered the true meaning of hell. No man should be asked to endure this sort of torture.

"Don't let me squash you," he said tautly, his control threatening to shatter.

"I'm fine. Do you have enough covers?"

"It's great." What wasn't so good was the way her rounded thighs heated his buttocks, and his all too predictable reaction to the intimacy of their position. "We ought to get some sleep."

"Sure." Her cheek pressed warmly between his shoulder blades. "It's been a long day."

The night was likely to be even longer.

Julianne listened to the howl of the wind outside and the softer sound of Erich's breathing. By his actions, he'd made it abundantly clear he didn't want to make love to her again. She shouldn't have been surprised. He'd already told her goodbye. If she hadn't been kidnapped he no doubt would have been a man of his word. Their goodbye would have been permanent.

With a discouraged sigh, she snuggled into his warmth. She wished she could take him back to Minnesota to ward off next winter's freezing weather. After this, settling for an electric blanket would seem a distant second best.

His sense of obligation had forced him to rescue her, she realized with a troubling ache in her chest. And he was indeed a man who took his obligations seriously. Like caring for his sister when his mother had run away. A noble dragon who didn't want anything more to do with Julianne.

At some point she dozed off, only to wake with the feeling she'd been sleeping with a furnace turned on high. Vaguely she became aware she and Erich had shifted positions during the night. A large, warm hand was nuzzled under her blouse, gently palming her breast, and she smiled to herself. Maybe his subconscious wasn't as immune to her limited charms as his waking mind was.

As THE GRAY LIGHT of dawn crept into the shelter, Erich's body became sharply aware of Julianne's legs entwined with his. They were thigh to thigh, hip to hip, her soft curves pressing insistently against his muscular leg. His hand rested at the swell of her hips. If she'd been awake she would have felt the hard evidence of his arousal. But her breathing was even.

He didn't dare move. Or maybe he hesitated because he wanted to enjoy Julianne's closeness a moment more. This was the last time he'd hold her in his arms, he promised himself, accepting the torture that vow entailed. She'd return to the States and he to his mountains. It was better an ocean separated them than to have her suffer the burdens he was forced to carry. Those that had broken his mother.

As she sleepily shifted her position, need shot through him like a lightning bolt, stealing his breath away. He ordered himself to end the torment by leaving the sleeping bag. His body ignored the command. Instead he drew in a deep breath filled with her wildflower scent, like a meadow in spring, and he knew winter would fill his heart when she left Austria for good.

"Erich?"

Her tentative tone paralyzed him. Had she discovered his blatant state of arousal? Did that frighten her? Or even make her angry since he had abruptly terminated their relationship?

His answer came with the caress of her hand between his thighs. His body clenched ever more tightly. "Julianna, my God, I don't think—"

"For a dragon, you think too much." She fumbled with his zipper. "I want this to happen, Erich. Here in your mountains, in your cave, so I can take the memory home with me. Is that too much to ask?"

He raised up on one elbow. Her eyes were dark with desire, the memory of the first time they'd made love apparent in their depths. Her lips parted in renewed anticipation. Her memories became his, stoking his need with flames that licked sensitive nerve endings. His senses were reeling out of control.

The effort to deny her request brought beads of sweat to his forehead. Only a saint would refuse her invitation. No one had ever accused him of being that. "I can't promise you anything, Julianna."

"I haven't asked you to." Her gaze held steady on his. "All I want is for you to love me now. Tomorrow can wait."

With a groan, he claimed her lips and forgot all the reasons why Julianne could never be his. Reality would intrude soon enough. For now, he simply let it slip away in the pleasure of the moment.

He would give her the memory she asked for, one so keen no amount of time would be able to erase it for either of them.

Determined to hold back his own release as long as possible, he coaxed her toward the highest peaks of arousal she could tolerate without tumbling over the brink. Each bit of flesh he revealed by removing her clothing, he laved with his tongue, nipped with his teeth and caressed with his hands. She arched against him in response. Her sobs caught in her throat and he drew them from even greater depths.

"Erich, please . . ."

"Not yet, my Julianna. Not yet."

Her fingers tangled in his hair as he explored her most secret places hidden behind a silvery blond triangle of curls. Her legs quivered uncontrollably as he spread kisses along her inner thigh.

"It's like I'm on fire," she cried. "I'm burning up."

So was he. Yet he continued to delay their final satisfaction. The price he paid became an anguish of self-inflicted torment.

She writhed and squirmed as he finally settled between her thighs.

"Look at me," he ordered, his voice husky with his effort to remain under control. "I want to watch you go over the top."

Her smile wavered. "Make me soar, Erich. Beyond tomorrow. I never want to be afraid of heights again."

She arched up to him and it was her cry of pleasure as he buried his shaft in her moist, tight cavern that sent him plummeting out into space. No safety rope tethered him to reality. He uttered a guttural sound and threw back his head. Tension burst from within him in hot, heavy pulses as he drove himself inside her one more time.

Chapter Thirteen

"I wish we didn't have to go back to the village."

Sighing, Julianne sat on the edge of a low stone monolith in the witches' circle and sipped the cup of morning tea Erich had prepared. The damp snow had already begun to melt where the sun touched the meadow. Though the trail down the hill would probably still be muddy and slippery, it looked as if finding an excuse to stay in this enchanted place would be difficult to come by. Too bad she couldn't cast a spell that would keep them here forever.

She'd lied to Erich when she'd told him she only wanted a memory to take home with her. She wanted far more than that. But obviously that's all he was willing to give.

Though he'd certainly fulfilled his part of the bargain. Last night, or rather this morning, was one she wouldn't soon forget.

"I need to get back to talk with Frederick," Erich said as he strapped the rolled sleeping bag onto his backpack.

"Frederick?"

"I had him spy on the kidnapper."

"That old curmudgeon cooperated?"

"I needed him because he had the journal. Actually, he seemed pleased to be helping out—in addition to the fact that he realized his own future was at stake. I think he likes you."

She grinned. "I've always made a big hit with old men and little boys." She'd had some trouble with those in between, however.

"You ready to go?" He lifted his pack over one shoulder.

"Sure." It hurt that he didn't want to linger in this idyllic spot, but she was determined not to let her feelings show. "I imagine the Sisters will be worried, too."

"All the more reason I need to get you back to Schloss Lohr as soon as possible."

"Right," she mumbled, tossing aside the remnants of her morning tea.

On their hike down the mountain, Erich was solicitous, even taking her hand when they had to cross a particularly difficult spot. But he was more guide than lover, withdrawing to an emotional distance Julianne found thoroughly irritating and painful. After the intimacies they'd shared, it seemed unfair she meant so little to him.

It was her own darned fault, she realized. She'd been the one to seduce *him* in the sleeping bag, not the other way around.

AT THE DOOR to Schloss Lohr, Erna swept Julianne into her arms. "Ach, *Liëbling,* my darling, we have been so worried about you." Her silver gray hair was mussed as though she'd been too preoccupied to comb it that morning.

Olga added a bear hug of her own. "When Erich told us you had been kidnapped..." Her voice caught on the word.

"Dear Sister has been up baking since before dawn."

"I do that when I am anxious," Olga admitted with a teary smile. "I have nearly run us out of flour. There is not another raisin left in the house and only a cup or two of sugar. If you had been missing another hour, I fear I would have had to make an emergency shopping trip to the village."

Julianne laughed. "Thank you for worrying about me so, Olga. And you, too, Grandma. I was terrified at first, but after Erich arrived, I was in good hands." She glanced at him, remembering just how talented his hands were, along with his lips and tongue. A very skillful lover, she mused.

"Come inside, child. You, too, dear boy. Someone has to help us eat all those luscious sweets and breads Olga has baked."

"I need to see Frederick," Erich said as they entered the castle.

"Poor man paced the floor half the night," Erna said. "I do believe he is in the library napping. When he is weary, he snores loud enough to keep the whole household awake."

Giving Olga a kiss on the cheek, Julianne said, "Why don't you put on a pot of coffee and we'll be there in a few minutes. I want to hear what Frederick has to say about my kidnapper." The kidnapper's identity was paramount in her mind. For Erich's sake, she hoped Helene wasn't behind her abduction.

As promised, Julianne and Erich found the ghost of Schloss Lohr in the library. Or at least, based upon the window-rattling snoring, he was somewhere in the room.

"Frederick!" Erich called.

With a final snort, the old man materialized on the couch. His disheveled appearance suggested he'd had a long night.

"High time you brought that young woman back home," he barked. "In my day, keeping a woman out all night would mean we would celebrate a wedding in the morning."

Julianne felt the heat of a blush race to her cheeks. In a prior century, there would have been cause for a shotgun wedding. But not in today's world, she thought with a surprising amount of regret.

"Our delay was unavoidable," Erich said tautly. "What did you learn about the kidnapper?"

Frederick patted the journal that rested on an end table beside him. "That no-account Paul Werndl was the one who retrieved the journal from the church."

"Really?" Julianne asked, surprised despite the suspicions Erich had already cast on his sister and her boyfriend.

A muscle ticked in Erich's jaw. "Was my sister part of the scheme?"

"Not that I was able to discern. I followed him home, waited until he called you, then made my presence known. By the time I left, he was babbling incoherently and hiding under his bed." A smug smile tugged at the corners of his lips. "After the haunting I gave him, Herr Werndl will be having nightmares for years."

"Then my abductor wasn't Hans." At the time, that had been the obvious conclusion, but Julianne now realized it could just as easily have been Paul hiding behind the Krampas mask. She hadn't heard his voice, nor had she seen his car.

"Nevertheless, my sister must have been the one who told Paul about the journal."

"The videotape about toads came from L.A. a couple of days ago," Julianne said. "I took it to your house and gave it to Helene. She looked miserable. She may have passed that on to Paul, too."

"Very possibly." Erich paced across the room and stared with a troubled frown at the small fire burning on the grate. "I had not suspected Paul loved Helene enough to risk going to jail for the sake of clearing the Langlois name. I don't understand his reasoning."

"Maybe *love* wasn't his motive," Julianne suggested.

Erich raised his gaze to meet hers. He had the deepest blue eyes, she mused, suddenly struck by the way his spiky black lashes set off their color. She'd have to remember that detail when she was back home in the States, along with strong shape of his jaw and the way his hair brushed the top of his collar. There'd be so much she'd want to recall, no single image would suffice to remind her of the breadth of his shoulders, his lean hips and legs that went on forever. She shuddered at the thought of how time would fade the impressions of the man she'd grown to love, then realized centuries couldn't erase all that he had become to her.

"What other motive could Paul have?" he asked.

Frederick "humphed." "The same blasted reason Egon Berker stole the castle from me. *Greed!*"

"With all due regard, sir, Schloss Lohr is old and needs substantial repairs. Its value is marginal, at best."

"Depending upon what you wanted to use it for," Julianne observed, though neither man paid her any attention.

"Blast and damnation!" Frederick came to his feet in a huff. "It is the *land* that has value, young pup! The crux of the matter has always been the land."

"The tenants pay little enough rent. It hardly seems—" Spearing his fingers through his hair, Erich recalled a dozen conversations he'd had with his sister about Paul. Each one scrolled through his mind like a looping videotape. Again and again he heard the words "ambitious" and "investors."

Grim understanding settled into his gut. "Paul was trying to gain control of the castle lands through Helene so he could develop them. At the expense of the tenants, would be my guess."

"Hallelujah! There may be hope for you yet, boy."

He shot his ancestor a quelling look. "Do you know what he was planning?"

"His quarters were cluttered with drawings of the Lohr valley obscenely crisscrossed by newfangled ski lifts and gondolas. I would say his nefarious schemes include the destruction of Lohr am See as we know it."

"Now wait a minute," Julianne protested. "Developing skiing facilities would bring in the tourist trade and therefore more employment opportunities. Would that be so awful?"

"A disaster," Frederick announced staunchly.

"Some of the neighboring valleys have tried to lure tourists their way by adding more skiing facilities," Erich explained. "In recent years, developers have attracted capital from all over Europe, spent other people's money while overbuilding, then taken their profits and left the villagers with ugly views, empty chair lifts and vacant hotel rooms. The mortgages have come close to bankrupting several small towns."

"Oh, I didn't realize... Do you think your sister knew what Paul was up to?" Julianne asked.

"I certainly hope she wasn't letting herself be used that way. But I'm damn well going to find out."

"I'll go with you," Julianne offered.

"This is a family matter."

"I'm the one who got kidnapped, remember? I think I have some right to know why."

"Listen to her, boy. She has more intelligence in her little finger than—"

"I said no!" Erich scowled at Frederick, who simply shrugged as if he hadn't said anything wrong.

Julianne shook her head. "You two gentlemen certainly appear to have pigheadedness in common. Behave yourself, Frederick, or I'll tell Erna you're acting up." Regretfully, she didn't have any similar leverage to make Erich take heed.

The old man's eyes widened. "There, what did I tell you? She is a smart one, that little wisp of a girl."

Erich whirled and headed for the door. "I don't need to be insulted by a cantankerous old man who's been dead for a hundred and fifty years. Or by you, Ms. Olson."

In spite of his stinging words, Julianne hurried after him. She understood he was concerned about his sister's involvement in her kidnapping but she simply couldn't let him walk out the door.

Before he reached the end of the hallway, she caught up with him. "I wasn't insulting you, Erich. I think Frederick is quite nice at heart, and there is something about him that definitely reminds me of you."

Cocking an eyebrow, Erich halted at the door. "Not my disposition, I trust."

"There are certain similarities." She smiled, then sobered. Where was the gentle, caring man who had made love to her only hours ago? "I can't believe Helene was actually involved in plotting my kidnapping with Paul. I know she's young, but—"

"Do you always see the goodness in people?"

"I try to. Is there anything wrong with that?"

"Just that you must be disappointed a good deal of the time."

Julianne didn't think so. Granted she'd been burned a few times, particularly when it came to matters of the heart. But as a rule people lived up to her expectations.

She supposed, given Erich's past, he'd learned a different lesson.

She wanted to be angry at him for not seeing beyond the limitations of his history, but she couldn't muster a single speck of self-righteous rage. He carried his own special burdens as well as any man did and better than most.

At some instinctive level she thought a man like Erich, who was so generous when he made love, could also learn to trust others. But she'd be leaving soon. Only a week remained before she had to use her return airline ticket or forfeit the price. There wouldn't be time for her to teach him, and at that thought sharp regret slid through her.

He rested his hand on the doorknob. "I have to go, Julianne. This is something I need to do alone."

"All right, but remember when you talk to Helene that even if she was involved, no great harm was done. I'm fine, thanks to you rescuing me, and the journal is safely back in Frederick's hands."

"I'll keep that in mind."

His gaze settled on Julianne's lips. For an instant she thought he was going to kiss her, then the slow closing of his eyes telegraphed the message that he had reconsidered.

"Julianne, about this morning..." He cleared his throat as though the words weren't coming easily. "I'm sorry. There is no way I can give you all that you deserve. I wish..." His thought remained unfinished as he whirled and walk out of the castle.

Julianne would never know what he had wished for.

A sense of finality and a feeling of dread settled in her chest as she watched him walk to his car. Unless she ran after him and forced her way into Erich's heart and his life, she was never going to see him again. As a matter of pride, she wouldn't do that. Love should be freely given, not thrust on a man through some sense of obligation.

Refusing to watch his car drive out of sight, she turned and went back to the library. Frederick was squatting next to the fireplace.

"What are you doing?" she asked.

"Destroying the evidence." He ripped several pages from the open journal and tossed them into the fire. The edges of the paper curled, then burst into flames. "I only waited to be sure you were safe."

"The journals represent your entire life's work. You can't burn them all."

"Only this one is incriminating. The rest will prove dull reading for my descendants, but I will leave them intact."

Frederick's descendants. Erich's children and grandchildren.

A lump formed in Julianne's throat at the thought of dark haired babies with beautiful blue eyes. Children she'd never see, never have a chance to hold in her arms and nurture as a mother should. Children she and Erich could have created together.

"Oh, damn..." she swore. Unshed tears stung at the back of her eyes.

Frederick glanced up from his task and made a derisive sound. "I have in mind to give that young pup a good thrashing. Shame on him for breaking the heart of such a pretty girl."

"It's not his fault. I'm the one who should have known better than to get involved in a one-sided vacation romance." She straightened her shoulders. "I'll get over it."

"Ah, yes, that may be true. But will *he* recover?" Frederick questioned enigmatically.

Frowning, Julianne left Frederick to the small bonfire he was feeding with sheets of paper. She intended to go tell the Sisters there'd be no Erich to help eat Olga's baked goods. But instead she found herself pacing the length of the long hallways of Schloss Lohr. She stopped at one door after another to rooms that had been closed off for perhaps a century. She knew the upper floors contained the same number of empty rooms.

A pity, she thought, not for the first time. With a modest amount of upgrading—including new plumbing—the castle would make a wonderful inn. It certainly had a colorful ambience, along with terrific views from almost every window. *Plus* a resident ghost. A great marketing combination, she mused, smiling.

As far as Julianne was concerned, her grandmother's instincts had been right on track about converting the castle to a small hotel. It'd be perfect. Too bad Erna and Olga had lacked the necessary experience and training to make it a successful venture.

With an abrupt halt, she stopped in front of the crossed swords.

Developing unneeded ski areas might not be the right answer for the economic woes of Lohr am See, but tourists certainly could be.

Mountain climbers.

Erich had trekked off to Salzburg to pick up his party of climbers. They could just as easily have stayed at an inn in Lohr am See, both before and after their trip, if there'd been suitable accommodations available.

Her mind raced with possibilities, ideas she was sure her grandmother would approve. Special weekends for young people, like a climbing camp. Perfect, given the Sister's youthful spirit and Erich's interest in teaching youngsters. Or tours for families with children, moms and dads and kids all learning together. The experts would find their own challenges, too, but they wouldn't have to leave wives and youngsters at some impersonal hotel far from their destination. It was all a question of marketing your services in the right way to the right audience. That's what she'd learned when she studied hotel management, and it still held true.

Excitement raced through her and she all but jumped up and clicked her heels together.

With the Sister's help and approval, she could make Lohr am See a mecca for both expert and beginning climbers. She wasn't doing this for Erich—though she hoped he would approve of the idea, too.

The fact was, she wanted this for herself. Her very own inn to run as she pleased, with no boss to answer to—except the Sisters, of course—and a way to help the villagers where her ancestors had lived. Ever since she'd arrived in Lohr am See, she'd felt an emotional attachment to the village and its people. Now she'd found a way to give back to her mother's homeland and maybe make up for how much she missed her mother.

ERICH PARKED his car next to Helene's behind their cottage. He wasn't looking forward to the confrontation with his sister. But he needed to know the truth.

As soon as he stepped through the back door, Helene burst into the kitchen. "Erich! I have been worried sick. You were due home yester—"

She stopped midsentence when he dropped his backpack heavily on the kitchen table. "Did you and Paul expect me to let Julianne freeze to death at the witches' circle?"

Eyes wide, her gaze shot from the pack back to Erich. "I don't know what you're talking about. You were guiding some climbers—"

"Where were you last night, Helene?"

"I was right here. Where else would I—"

"You weren't here when I got home. And you weren't here when I left after dark. I want to know where you were."

"I know what you are thinking, but you are wrong. I didn't spend the night with Paul." A flush stained her cheeks. "If you must know, I was furious with you. So I went to visit my friend Maria Schlager in Thumersbach. I was back by nine, but you were not—"

"You didn't see Paul last night?"

"No. He said he had some business to do." With a shake of her head, she flipped the ends of her dark hair behind her shoulder. "Not that it's any business of yours, big brother. I am old enough to—"

"Did you tell Paul about Frederick's journal?"

"Why are you quizzing me like I am some sort of a criminal? Of course I told Paul. I had to. For your information, he said that your decision to ignore your family history won't make any difference. He still plans to marry me, no thanks to you." She jutted her chin up at a stubborn angle.

Erich wanted to take her by the shoulders and shake some sense into her.

"Maybe Paul's still willing," he said tautly, "because he tried to take matters into his own hands. Because of what he did, Julianne might have died. Now, the thing I want to know, Helene, is how deeply you have been involved in his whole scheme. Or was he only using you?"

She paled and backed away.

Erich intended to learn the whole truth, no matter the cost to himself or his sister. Then he'd talk to the police.

THE NEXT MORNING Julianne was sitting in the castle kitchen, papers covered with notes and computations spread out all over the table. Ideas had spun through her head all night until there was no hope of sleeping. So, since before dawn, she'd been writing and figuring until the plans had taken on a life of their own.

Of course, she'd need her grandmother's approval, but she could practically see the crowds flocking to Schloss Lohr and smell breakfast cooking in the oven for the guests at the inn. Olga would make the perfect pastry chef. Her mouth watered at the thought.

The image wavered when she heard a knock on the back door.

Thinking it might be Erich, Julianne's heart did a little flipflop. Then she realized he always came to the front door. Disappointed, she tucked her pencil behind her ear and went to see who was there.

Wild-eyed, her hair in disarray, Helene stood on the back stoop. "I hope you are pleased with yourself!"

"Pleased?"

"Paul has been arrested. And it is all your fault."

"How can that be? I haven't even talked to the police yet. And no one's come by to question me."

"He confessed," Helene wailed. "And he has been babbling about being attacked by a *pillow!* They have locked him up in jail and it is all your fault."

"Helene, the man kidnapped me. How can that be my fault? He broke the law."

"So now neither of us will marry. I cannot have Paul, but you will not get Erich, either. Even if he does love you."

Julianne's heart did something strange and fluttery, as if it had been given an electric shock. Lord, she needed to go jogging more often so her cardiovascular system would be in better condition, not the casualty of every little emotional upheaval. "He loves me?" she echoed.

"Why else do you think he has made such a fool of himself? Schloss Lohr could have been ours. Erich's and mine! And he gave it all away because of you."

Helene sobbed a hiccuppy sound and tears overflowed. "And now we have nothing and he is going to send me away. To Salzburg," she cried.

"Come inside, Helene." Julianne put a sympathetic arm around the young woman's shoulders. "There's coffee on and more sweet rolls than an army could eat."

"I do not want to—"

"I think you need someone to talk to. Big brothers aren't real good for that. And I certainly have a few questions for you. Come on."

Julianne got her inside and settled down with a cup of coffee. The poor girl was an emotional wreck. Helene must have been devastated to learn Paul had only been using her, and she still wasn't quite ready to give up the fantasy of what she had thought was love.

Her chin quivered. "I will never marry," Helene vowed. "Not that any man would ever want me."

"Of course they will. You're a beautiful girl."

"I am not."

"I imagine if you cut your hair a little shorter and pulled it back like this..." Julianne demonstrated, remembering the texture of Erich's hair. "Then with a touch of eye shadow, you'd be truly striking."

Still skeptical, Helene frowned.

"Trust me, in another year or so, there won't be a man in all of Austria who will be able to resist you."

"You think so?" She sniffled and blew her nose on the tissue Julianne had provided.

"I suspect if you go to that art school in Salzburg, as Erich has suggested, you'll find more men interested than you can beat off with a stick. And all of them will be far more honorable than Paul Werndl."

"But I wanted him . . ."

"You wanted to have a man love you. Paul was trying to *use* you. That's a very different situation." Julianne had had similar experiences, and it always hurt to learn the truth.

"Well..." With a thoughtful expression, Helene tore off a dainty bite of sweet roll and popped it into her mouth.

"Now, then," Julianne said, sensing Helene's improved mood and filled with her own questions, "if you think Erich loves me, why wouldn't he want to marry me?" Because the thought had certainly crossed *her* mind.

"Because he knows being a Langlois is too hard on a woman. It drove our mother away. And look what it has done to me!" she wailed, agitated again.

"What did it do to you, Helene?"

"I don't have any friends in the village. Nobody ever talks to me. They call me names. It's awful!"

"Did you ever try to be a friend to them, Helene? Or did you *expect* them to hate you, so you intentionally stayed apart from the villagers."

Helene set her jaw again. "I do not know what you are talking about."

"When that climber was trapped on the mountain, Erich thought the villagers wouldn't want his help to rescue the young man. He wasn't going to offer his assistance, even though he's the best guide in the whole region. And the fact was, they were eager for him to be a part of the operation." She covered Helene's hand. "To have a friend, you have to be one first."

"I don't know..."

Sometimes it took a while to absorb that lesson, so Julianne returned to her more immediate concern. "At the very least, Erich ought to realize I'm a very different person than either you or your mother. A few people calling me a witch wouldn't make any difference to how I felt about him." Granted, she wasn't pleased with the prospect of overcoming any lingering animosity among the villagers, but she could handle it.

"It's not just how you would be treated. Some day you are going to *own* a castle, and he has nothing to offer a woman but our old cottage to live in. It is a horrible place. So dingy and dirty. He says you deserve more than that."

"I do?" A dragon's cave would be fine with her, if the right dragon asked her. "He must not think very much of me if he believes I'd only want to marry a man who has lots of money."

"Oh, he thinks you are *perfect!* While I am a..." She sniffled again. "A rotten, spoiled child."

Smiling, Julianne patted her hand. "Maybe there is a way we can both prove him wrong, Helene."

Mentally, she squared her shoulders and straightened her spine. She wasn't going to walk away with a broken heart this time the way she had in Minnesota. Nor was she going to let Erich stroll out of her life the same way he had strolled in. Not without a fight.

But how, she wondered, could a woman convince a man that love would be enough?

The only answer that popped into her mind scared her half to death.

SHE WASN'T AFRAID of heights. She'd been telling herself that lie for the past three days, while she got the rest of her plans in order.

Sweaty palms didn't mean a thing. Her love for Erich would give her all the courage she needed.

She'd left Schloss Lohr at dawn to collect the one symbol of love she felt Erich couldn't ignore—when it came from her. A sprig of edelweiss that grew at the highest, *scariest* elevations in the Alps.

Surely he'd realize this was a true gift from the heart, risking her neck on a narrow path that lead up into the clouds.

But by the time the sun was fully up, Julianne had shed her lightweight jacket and tied it around her waist. The trail narrowed even more, until she had to place one foot in front of the other as if she were walking a straight line for a sobriety test. She steadied herself with one sweaty palm on the nearly vertical cliff beside her.

"Don't look down," she warned herself, pausing to catch her breath. Her legs were already trembling and not entirely from fatigue.

She looked up, craning her neck to get a glimpse of her destination. The summit looked impossibly high and unattainable except by the alpine birds soaring near the peak. She wouldn't have to go quite that far, she assured herself. Only to the first patch of edelweiss. A single sprig would do.

She might not have the nerve to deliver her offer of love directly to Erich—it would be too awful if he rejected the gift to her face—but she'd thought of the perfect messenger.

Glancing to see where she could safely take her next step on the trail, a dizzying sensation of losing her equilibrium swept over her. Sweat broke out on her forehead. Her stomach heaved.

"Oh, God, please don't let me fall..."

Chapter Fourteen

The door to Erich's workroom blew open with a crash. Before he could react with so much as a curse, Frederick materialized in the middle of the room, his face an apoplectic shade of red.

"She has gone mad, I tell you!" he bellowed. "Absolutely insane. You must stop her at once before matters get entirely out of hand."

Scowling, Erich set aside the climbing rope he'd been checking for abrasions. "Who's gone mad? What the devil are you talking about, old man?"

"That little wench Julianne has turned traitor! She will ruin the village and destroy Schloss Lohr if she has her way."

The painful ache Erich had been carrying around in his chest for the past three days intensified. It had been that long since he'd seen Julianne, an agony of endless days and sleepless nights. "Julianne's activities are no concern of mine. At any rate, she will be returning to America soon."

"She is not leaving. She is staying here, at Schloss Lohr, and the last of the damnable Berkers will finally destroy everything I have worked so hard to maintain."

"She's staying?" He exhaled the words in a rush, as though the air had been forcefully expelled from his lungs. He didn't know whether to be exhilarated or angry that she was staying in the village where her presence would taunt him with all he wanted and couldn't have.

"What is worse, she has called a meeting of the villagers this evening at the church so they can approve her plans. Fools that they are, they will no doubt cheer her on." Clutching a sprig of edelweiss that looked freshly cut, he waved it at Erich. "Mark my words, all will be lost. My life in ruins..."

Distracted, Erich stared at the small bouquet. "Where did you get those flowers?"

The ghost of Schloss Lohr looked at his hand as though he had forgotten he carried the small treasure, a romantic symbol of love that Erich had rejected as meaningless. Until now.

"Julianne coerced me into delivering these weeds to you. I imagine she foolishly thought if I brought them to you, you would attend the meeting and support her devilish scheme. I told her you were smarter than that."

"If you were mad at her, why would you do what she asked?"

"Because she is damned persuasive, that's why. And I want you to put an end to this nonsense."

"Where did she get the flowers?" A woman who was terrified of heights couldn't have climbed on her own to the peaks where edelweiss grew. She would have been too frightened, unless...

"How should I know where this sprig came from?" Frederick grumbled. "There has been so much secretive planning going on at the castle between that girl and the Sisters, it has given me a headache. The chit left early this morning, without so much as a by-your-leave. She reappeared this afternoon, looking a fright, with a smug grin and this silly souvenir from some jaunt up the mountains—"

"Julianne went climbing? On her own?" Impossible, Erich thought, even though the evidence was right in front of his eyes. Yet he couldn't quite be sure what it meant. Indeed, he was afraid to hope.

"Good grief, man, are you not listening? The whole future of Schloss Lohr is at stake and all you can think about is a sprig of edelweiss. The meeting is starting within the hour. You must stop her. She has gotten it into her head that if Werndl was capable of finding investors for the development of the Lohr valley, so is she."

"For a ski area?" A stunning possibility that Julianne must know went against all that Erich believed was right for the area. Perhaps this was her own style of retribution.

"What do the details matter? She is going to turn my beloved Schloss Lohr into an *inn* for tourists. Do you realize how much work that will entail for *me?* I will never get a full night's sleep again." Wearily, Frederick lowered himself onto the stool beside Erich's work-bench and buried his head in his hands. "If you have any respect for me, if the blood running through your veins is truly Langlois blood, you must stop her."

Erich wasn't entirely sure what to make of Frederick's nearly hysterical account of what was about to happen at the village church. But he was sure he needed to see Julianne. An invitation delivered in the form of a sprig of edelweiss couldn't be ignored.

Even by a cynic who had never believed in love.

"ARE YOU SURE we are doing the right thing, sister?"

Erna smoothed the last of the wrinkles from the wedding gown her daughter had worn twenty-eight years ago, the same simple dress she hoped her grand-daughter would be wearing that very evening. "The villagers will all be at the church. It seems a perfect time for a wedding, do you not agree?"

"But we are not even sure Erich will come to the church. And Julianne knows nothing about—"

"Stuff and nonsense. I do not believe in long en-gagements." Erna slipped the dress onto a hanger and smiled at her handiwork. "Those two young people are in love. We simply need to give them a little nudge and then strike when the iron is hot, so to speak."

"I do so hope you are right." Olga placed the last of several dozen cookies she had baked into a cookie tin to be carried to the church. "Frederick did not seem at all pleased with Julianne's plans for the castle."

"Dearest Frederick is too much a fussbudget. Turn-ing Schloss Lohr into an inn will be wonderful fun. And it will be lovely to have Julianne living here. Maybe there will even be a great-grandchild for me to hold before too long."

"Oh, mercy," Olga giggled. "Whatever will Frederick do with dirty baby nappies in his castle?"

Their eyes met in gleeful conspiracy and youthful laughter filled the kitchen at Schloss Lohr.

FOR THE THIRD TIME in as many minutes, Julianne checked the charts she'd drawn. She'd diagramed advertising costs, anticipated room occupancy rates, potential revenues and increased employment opportunities. By big-city standards, her concept was quite small. But for Lohr am See it would mean a major investment of both money and manpower. The villagers had a right to know the costs. And the risks.

If they went along with her ideas, she'd proceed to develop funding sources both locally and in the States. If not, she'd give it all up.

In any event, she really wished Erich would show up to give his blessing.

She had risked a huge amount by sending him that sprig of edelweiss. Including risking her neck on that narrow, slippery path to the top of Riemannhaus.

As terrified as she'd been making her way up—and down—the mountain on her own, she was even more afraid Erich would reject the love she'd offered. Surely her message had been clear, even if the messenger had been a bit unorthodox.

The door to the church swung open and Julianne glanced up. Though the lighting was dim, she would have known those broad shoulders and lean hips anywhere in the world.

Emotion tightened a lump in her throat. "I was afraid you wouldn't come."

His expression shadowed, he walked down the center aisle toward her. His footsteps echoed heavily on the quarried stone floor and the ancient wooden pews stood as mute witnesses to her fears. The scent of fragrant candle wax hung with cloying sweetness in the air, the light flickering on pillars hewn from the mountains that surrounded Lohr am See.

Julianne found she couldn't draw a breath. These next few moments would set the course for the rest of her life. Her heart began to accelerate and her palms began to sweat as if she were standing at the edge of a precipice.

"I have so many questions, I don't even know where to begin." His voice was raspy with emotion, his eyes dark with feeling.

She ordered her lungs to function and took a deep breath. "The answer to every one of your questions is that I love you. It doesn't matter to me what your name is, or if you own a cottage or a castle. I want to spend the rest of my life with you. If you'll have me."

"The edelweiss?"

"It was the only way I could be sure you'd believe me."

"But you're terrified of heights."

"Absolutely. Though maybe a little less so now than I used to be. But I'm even more afraid of losing you."

A candle sputtered in the silence and flickered out, reducing the light by a minuscule amount. Erich's skeptical look remained undimmed.

"You say you love me, but you're still going to turn Lohr am See into a ski area? Knowing my feelings on the subject, how can you make plans to scar the mountains with cuts through the forest and ugly cables for chair lifts?"

She raised her eyebrows. "Not skiing, Erich. If the villagers agree—and I've already talked to several of them—Lohr am See will be a mountain climbing mecca for both beginners and experts. A base of operations that won't leave a single mark on the landscape."

One side of his lips twitched into a half smile that did something warm and wonderful to her insides. "Frederick said—"

"Frederick has been very distraught lately. I think he doesn't adjust well to change."

"I imagine not. He said something about turning the castle into an inn."

"It's what I've always wanted, to run a small hotel on my own. Some of the farmers will turn their extra rooms into guest rooms, and the Boar's Head Pub is thinking about expanding into a small, quality hotel."

"You've done all this in three days?" he asked incredulously.

"Once I make up my mind about something, I don't know how to slow down."

He chuckled, a warm, raspy sound. "And I'm part of the plan?"

"I was certainly hoping you'd approve."

The church door opened and half a dozen chatting villagers entered the chapel.

Erich caught Julianne's hand. "I think we need to continue our discussion in a little more privacy."

"But I invited the villagers to—"

"They can wait." Tugging her along, he pulled her into the vestry, which contained a small desk and cabinets that lined one wall. He cupped her face between his large, gentle hands. "Do you have any idea what you'd be letting yourself in for if we were to marry? You'd be a Langlois—"

"And proud of it." Her heart leapt at his mention of marriage.

"The villagers would—"

"I can handle the villagers, Erich. Most of them are already my friends. What I wouldn't be able to manage is you hiding out in your cave when things got difficult. I'm not so naive as to believe love is enough to make a relationship work without a great deal of effort. I'm willing to go the extra mile."

"Or climb a mountain?"

"I'd do it again if I had to. A hundred times." Though she doubted she'd ever get completely past her fear of heights, the climb had been an exhilarating experience. The moment she'd wrapped her fingers around the edelweiss, she'd felt a great surge of satisfaction. She'd overcome mind-numbing terror to reach her goal and felt good about it. For her, that was enough. From now on she'd be willing to leave the serious mountain climbing to Erich.

"I don't deserve a woman like you."

"*Deserve* has nothing to do with it, Erich. Love happens. It appears when and where you least expect it. Like an avalanche, there's no way you can stop it once it gets started."

He brushed a kiss to the top of her head. Her hair was like silk and smelled of sweet wildflowers. No matter how long he lived, the scent would remind him of Julianne and his need for her. He couldn't let her go. These last few days had proved he wasn't strong enough to make that large a sacrifice. Knowing she loved him, knowing she had challenged her fears to prove that love, was his undoing.

His heart seemed to stop as the realization settled into his bones, into his *heart*. Since he'd been a little boy pleading with his father to go after his mother, to bring her back, he'd never expected to find love. To *be* loved.

It took him a moment to realize that the hard, aching emptiness he'd been carrying around in his chest since his mother had left had been filled. Not just this minute, but since Julianne had entered his life. The *föhn* wind that was her smile, her determination, her generosity, had been healing that childish wound without him being aware of her curative powers. Why hadn't he noticed? How had he been so blind?

"I should have been the one to bring *you* edelweiss, Julianna. It's a man's place—"

"Not when he doesn't believe in romance."

"I do now, my sweet, determined Julianna. And every day for the rest of my life, I will be grateful you have taught me how to love."

"Oh, Erich . . ." Tears sprang to her eyes.

She stood on tiptoe and he captured her lips in a kiss that sealed his promise for all eternity. In giving of herself so willingly, Erich could do nothing less.

Emotions he'd kept in check for all of his life burst over him, rocking him from his arrogant pedestal, and he pulled her into his arms. The tears he had refused to shed when his mother had deserted him, the stoic shield he had built for himself through all the years of ostracism and harassment, crumbled like a poorly built wall of stone.

"It seems the dragon may have come down from the mountain to steal a virgin, but in return she has stolen his heart. Marry me, Julianna. Be my wife and stay by my side forever."

"Yes, Erich, oh, yes..."

The door to the vestry burst open.

"Oh, dear, we do hope we are not interrupting," Erna said, popping into the room.

"Of course we are *interrupting,* sister. It is just what we had in mind."

"Well, yes, but you must not—"

"Ladies! Julianna and I came in here to gain a little privacy."

"I know that, sweet boy." Erna patted him on the cheek then smiled at Julianne. "That is why we brought the wedding gown along."

"My mother's wedding dress?" Julianne's voice rose in surprise.

"And I have Erich's best suit." Smiling more broadly than he'd seen his sister smile in a long time, Helene followed the Sisters into the room. She'd done something different with her hair, and a touch of makeup emphasized her eyes, making her startlingly attractive. He shot Julianne a puzzled glance, suspecting she was at the root of his sister's make-over.

He slid a possessive arm around Julianne. "What's going on here?" he questioned her and the gathering crowd.

Eyes sparkling, Julianne said, "I think my grandmother and Olga are outdoing themselves at matchmaking."

"It does seem as though the whole of Lohr am See is at the church this evening," Erna explained as she hung the gown over the door of a cabinet. "We thought this would be a good time for a wedding."

"An excellent time," Olga agreed.

"Now?" Julianne asked, wide-eyed. "But we haven't had a chance to—"

With a painful choking sound, Frederick materialized in the middle of the room. "Don't let them do this to you, son. These women will wrap you around their collective little fingers and there will be no hope to stop the ruination of Schloss Lohr."

Erich's head spun. "I don't think anyone is planning to ruin—"

"An inn! There will be tourists in every room with their newfangled electrical contraptions. They will burn the place down, not to mention the messes they will leave behind." Arms waving, Frederick continued to rant his various objections to Julianne's plan.

Julianne's barely suppressed laughter rippled through Erich. "You know what I think?" he asked softly as the Sisters tried to refute Frederick's objections.

She sputtered, "Th-that you're being railroaded?"

"That whatever happens, I'm going to take you home with me tonight and make love to you until dawn. It seems to me you have a choice of doing that as my wife, or not. But the result will be absolutely the same. I'm never going to let you go."

A radiant smile danced in her eyes. "Then I suppose getting married would be the wisest course. I wouldn't want to shock the Sisters by doing anything that would cause gossip in the village."

"Oh, Julianne," Helene cried, "I am so happy for you. Both of you. I wonder...I mean...well, if you thought you needed a maid of honor..."

Julianne gave Helene's hand a squeeze. "I can't think of anything I'd like more than to have you stand up with me. We are going to be sisters, after all."

The girl's enthusiasm bubbled up into a fountain of happy tears.

With mock gruffness, Erich commented, "Does that mean I'm supposed to ask Frederick to be my best man?"

Smiling sweetly, she said, "Well, he is the one who brought us together."

Erich rolled his eyes. Maybe his ancestor was right. Fighting the Berker clan was a lost cause, one he intended to lose as many times as possible.

AS IF SHE'D BEEN caught in the middle of a whirlwind, within half an hour Julianne found herself standing in front of the altar exchanging wedding vows with the man she had come to love so desperately. She wore the same gown her mother had worn and stood in the same holy place, filled with the same joy all of the Berker women must have felt as they committed to a lifetime of love.

Looking up at the three stained-glass windows behind the altar, she felt so close to her mother she could almost hear her good wishes, like a whispered lullaby that eased her loss.

The priest said, "And do you have a ring for this woman?"

"Ring?" Erich questioned. "This has all happened so fast."

"I have it, young pup." As if by magic, a gold ring appeared. An invisible Frederick passed it to the groom. "At least I had enough foresight to retrieve a suitable ornament from the castle. You don't deserve her, you know."

"Yes, I know," Erich whispered ardently, "but I shall always cherish her. I swear that on the proud name of Langlois."

"Amen," Frederick agreed. His voice was thick, as though there were tears clogging his throat.

Julianne raised her gaze to meet Erich's. Her heart expanded with the love she felt. He looked so stern, so serious as he spoke the words that would bind them together, yet she knew beneath his forbidding veneer he was capable of the deepest kind of emotion and unending loyalty.

The dragon had indeed come down from the mountain. Julianne had every intention of keeping him there for a long, long time.

BRIDE'S BAY RESORT

UNLOCK THE DOOR TO GREAT ROMANCE AT BRIDE'S BAY RESORT

Join Harlequin's new across-the-lines series, set in an exclusive hotel on an island off the coast of South Carolina.

Seven of your favorite authors will bring you exciting stories about fascinating heroes and heroines discovering love at Bride's Bay Resort.

Look for these fabulous stories coming to a store near you beginning in January 1996.

Harlequin American Romance #613 in January
Matchmaking Baby by Cathy Gillen Thacker

Harlequin Presents #1794 in February
Indiscretions by Robyn Donald

Harlequin Intrigue #362 in March
Love and Lies by Dawn Stewardson

Harlequin Romance #3404 in April
Make Believe Engagement by Day Leclaire

Harlequin Temptation #588 in May
Stranger in the Night by Roseanne Williams

Harlequin Superromance #695 in June
Married to a Stranger by Connie Bennett

Harlequin Historicals #324 in July
Dulcie's Gift by Ruth Langan

Visit Bride's Bay Resort each month wherever Harlequin books are sold.

HARLEQUIN ®

BBAYG

Yo amo novelas con corazón!

Starting this March, Harlequin opens up to a whole new world of readers with two new romance lines in SPANISH!

Harlequin Deseo
- passionate, sensual and exciting stories

Harlequin Bianca
- romances that are fun, fresh and very contemporary

With four titles a month, each line will offer the same wonderfully romantic stories that you've come to love—now available in Spanish.

Look for them at selected retail outlets.

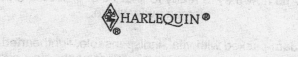

HARLEQUIN ®

The Magic Wedding Dress

Imagine a wedding dress that costs a million dollars. Imagine a wedding dress that allows the wearer to find her one true love—not always the man she thinks it is. And then imagine a wedding dress that brings out all the best attributes in its bride, so that every man who glimpses her is sure to fall in love. Karen Toller Whittenburg imagined just such a dress and allowed it to take on a life of its own in her new American Romance trilogy, *The Magic Wedding Dress*. Be sure to catch all three:

March
#621—THE MILLION-DOLLAR BRIDE

May
#630—THE FIFTY-CENT GROOM

August
#643—THE TWO-PENNY WEDDING

Come along and dream with Karen Toller Whittenburg!

HARLEQUIN®

AMERICAN ◆ ROMANCE®

In Name Only

...because there are many reasons for saying "I do."

American Romance cordially invites you to a
wedding of convenience. This is one reluctant bride
and groom with their own unique reasons for
marrying...IN NAME ONLY.

By popular demand American Romance continues this
story of favorite marriage-of-convenience books. Don't
miss

#624 THE NEWLYWED GAME
by Bonnie K. Winn
March 1996

Find out why some couples marry first...and learn to
love later. Watch for IN NAME ONLY!